THE TRANSFORMERS

MORE THAN MEETS THE EYE!

™

AUTOBOT   DECEPTICON

◆ Compiled and edited by Sheila Cranna.   ◆ Designed by Steve Cook.

This book belongs to ....

THE TRANSFORMERS™ ANNUAL published by MARVEL COMICS LTD., 23 Redan Place, London W2 4SA, in association with GRANDREAMS LTD., Jadwin House, 205-211 Kentish Town Road, London NW5. THE TRANSFORMERS (including all prominent characters featured) and the distinctive likenesses thereof are the trademarks of HASBRO INDUSTRIES INC. and copyright © 1986 by HASBRO INDUSTRIES INC. All rights reserved.

IN THE BEGINNING...

(THE STORY OF THE TRANSFORMERS... *SO FAR.*)

The conflict has stretched over millions of years, traversing the great gulfs of space from its origins on the gleaming metal world of Cybertron to its current shape and form, here on our own planet – Earth. Join us now as we take a privileged look at the course of this conflict to date; the battles fought, the many and varied characters involved, and the victories, defeats, losses and gains made by both the heroic Autobots and the evil Decepticons. In fact, join young computer wizard, Adam Reynolds as he accidentally unlocks the secret of the vast Decepticon computer – entering a world beyond his (and your) imagination... the world of the TRANSFORMERS!

"Blast!" – Slumping his chin forward into one cupped hand, Adam Reynolds stared disconsolately at the four – now familiar – words that glowed green on his visual display unit, mocking his attempts to gain entry to the Portland National Bank's central computer. 'Incorrect code. Access denied.' They told him that for the twenty-fifth time this long night he had failed to outfox the various security devices installed to prevent unauthorised eyes gazing upon the bank's accounts.

It wasn't the money, he told himself for the twenty-fifth time, that was concerning him, rather the face he would lose with his fellow computer club members. When Tommy Ryde had bet him a dollar that he couldn't find out how much he had in his savings account, he had rashly risen to the challenge, claiming that there wasn't a computer in existence that he – and his trusty Sinclair – couldn't break into. Now, though, at a little past midnight he was more willing to admit his fallibility. Knitting his tired fingers and pushing them outwards until the joints clicked, he prepared himself for just one more try.

Those fingers danced briefly over the computer's push-button phone, connecting it instantly – through a phone link – to the Portland National's computer, then moved to the Sinclair's keyboard, rapidly typing in instructions – skating with ease through the system's primary defences. . .

He froze, staring disbelievingly at the identification code that pulsed rhythmically in front of his eyes. With growing despair he realised that this wasn't the National's computer he'd accessed. Either in his haste, or due to his tiredness, he'd phoned the wrong computer!

It was the final straw. . . rage and frustration boiled over, and Adam slammed a hand down onto his keyboard – hard! The computer's anguished squeal was abruptly silenced as his V.D.U. erupted into life, spewing line upon line of information across its glowing screen. Adam's finger wavered over the Erase button, ready to break contact with this unknown computer. The finger remained where it was, as uninterested eyes slowly widened in amazement, and a sleepy mind suddenly found itself wide awake. The story unfolding on his screen read like a sci-fi movie, but with all that had happened in Oregon recently, he knew that science fiction was – in this case – science fact.

Hardly daring to tear his eyes from the screen, Adam groped blindly for the Printout button. The silence of his room was abruptly broken by the chatter of the tele-printer as the glowing words began to translate themselves to page upon page of typed information. . .

DECEPTICON MAINFRAME COMPUTER – DATALOG. . .

WAR-TAPE ONE: CYBERTRON TO EARTH.

Little is known of planet Cybertron's origins. Many have speculated but no hard facts have been produced. What *is* known is that at some point the machine-world of Cybertron evolved sentient machine beings, with the capacity to transform their robot form into vehicles, communication devices, and weapons. The Autobots – as these 'Transformers' named themselves – lived harmoniously with one another in peace and prosperity. But there were those who looked contemptuously on the peace-loving rulers of Cybertron, those who wanted power through conquest and destruction.

These rogue Autobots – led by Megatron – called themselves The Decepticons. When they had amassed enough followers and firepower, the Decepticons struck – cutting a swathe of chaos and carnage across Cybertron, destroying Autobot settlements with deadly precision. So vast was the power unleashed in these initial attacks that Cybertron was shaken loose from its orbit and sent plummeting through space. The war raged furiously across the runaway planet, and, though the Autobots fought valiantly, it was soon apparent that they could not hope to prevail against the Decepticon war-machine. Until, that is, a leader arose in the city-state of Iacon, to meld the Autobots into an awesome army, powerful enough to hold their own against the Decepticons. This Autobot was Optimus Prime. Using his ability to transform into a combat vehicle, Prime possessed a firepower potential that only Megatron could match.

The war continued unabated until a time when Cybertron's wayward course placed it directly in the path of an asteroid belt. The Autobots realised that Cybertron was doomed, unless they could construct a vast and powerful craft to propel a demolition team into space

ahead of the planet. While the Autobots laboured to build The Ark, the Decepticons were constructing their own spacecraft. Megatron, learning of the Autobots' plans, decided that as soon as the Autobots had cleared the danger from space, they would strike – destroying the weakened Autobots. The Ark performed her duties well, its vast weaponry pulverising a path through the space-born rocks. True to Megatron's plan, the Decepticons took advantage of the Autobots' exhaustion, attacking and boarding the Ark. Prime decided that the Ark must never fall into enemy hands and plotted a suicidal course into the third planet of the system they were passing through. The Ark crash-landed with crushing force, rendering all aboard – Autobot and Decepticon alike – inactive, and badly damaging the craft's computer systems.

Watching this planetfall from the Decepticon spacecraft was Shockwave – military operations officer – who had stayed behind to act as a possible back-up in case the attack on the Ark faltered. Shockwave assumed his space-gun mode and followed down to investigate. However, while passing through the radiation belts ringing the planet, his guidance systems malfunctioned, and he touched down half a world away from the Ark, in a region still inhabited by the Carbon-Based species known as dinosaurs.

Using the last of its power, the Ark's computers identified Shockwave's presence as a threat and re-constructed five Autobots to resemble dinosaurs, which its damaged sensors had perceived as the dominant mechanical life-form. These Dinobots – Grimlock, Snarl, Sludge, Slag and Swoop – travelled to the Savage Land – as it would later become known – and battled Shockwave. But Shockwave's power was second only to Megatron's, and he easily bested the Dinobots; condemning them to lie buried deep within a tar pit. A chance last strike by the Dinobots ensured that Shockwave joined them in their oblivion, buried under hundreds of tons of rock. The Transformers had come to Earth.

Tape one ends.

Further instructions or disconnect?

Adam typed in the word 'hold' and sat back heavily in his chair. It had to be a joke. Such beings couldn't possibly exist here on Earth, and yet. . .

Swinging round, he leafed rapidly through a rag-tag collection of well thumbed comics, magazines and newspapers until his excited eyes lighted upon a recent copy of the Portland Chronicle. The lead story told graphically of the giant robots which had, of late, become a regular feature in the lives of the population of Oregon and other nearby states. Robots which, if the newspaper's text was accurate, were controlled by a terrorist organisation run by a character called Robot-Master. Given a straight choice between believing that a guy, who looked as though he belonged in one of Adam's tawdrier science-fiction comics, was in control of the Transformers and that the robots were aliens, stranded on Earth, Adam knew which explanation he'd plump for. There was a simple way to check.

Turning back to his computer, Adam keyed in a request for information on Robot-Master. The response suggested he access something called DATAFILE. . .

(TURN TO PAGE 21)

Optimus Prime? Could such a being truly exist? Here on Earth – now? Questions careened wildly around Adam's mind as he studied the history of the Autobot leader for the fourth time. He forgot completely about Robot-Master as he speculated on the other treasures to be found within Datafile. Calling on his computer's memory, Adam scanned the first jumbled series of words his computer had plundered from Decepticons. Closer examination of the seemingly unconnected phrases reinforced Adam's theory that he'd accidentally discovered the computer's store of highly classified access codes – codes that would undoubtedly unlock the rest of the Decepticons' secrets. Taking the plunge, Adam began to ask the computer about the Decepticon leader – Megatron!

(TURN TO PAGE 33)

Disconnect? No – that's not what I want at all, thought Adam, rapidly contradicting his own instruction. Reason had screamed at him to cut and run with what he had discovered so far, but curiosity urged him to go deeper still into the Decepticons' storehouse of information. Throwing caution to the wind, Adam keyed in a rapid series of questions and sat back to wait as the computer pondered its answers.

Deep within the computer's central data core a logic chip acknowledged that one of the questions it had been asked had been preceded by an incorrect security rating. As per its programming, the computer began to oblige the user with correct answers to all the questions, while simultaneously preparing a charge of some 1,000,000 volts which it would shortly deliver to that selfsame user. . .

Question: How did the Transformers become re-animated?
Answer: For four million years the Autobots and Decepticons remained deactivated inside the Ark, which itself nestled within the shattered husk of the dormant volcano, Mount St. Hilary, until a freak eruption stirred the dormant circuits of the Ark's living computer. Aunty, as the computer was known, sent out recorder probes which identified Earthen machines as the dominant life-forms on this world, having learnt from its previous mistake with the Dinobots. It re-constructed all the wrecked Transformers aboard the Ark, regardless of whether they were Autobots or Decepticons, so that they had the capability to transform into a likeness of the Earthen vehicle, weapon or communications device that most closely corresponded to each's Cybertron form. The Decepticons were first to recover, and Megatron swiftly withdrew his troops from the Ark so that they could assess their position.

'250,000 volts and increasing,' the computer noted to itself as it prepared to answer the next question. . .

Question: Have any human beings become directly involved in the war? If yes, please supply details.
Answer: Yes. Following the initial clash between the Autobots and the Decepticons on Earth, the human known as Buster Witwicky inadvertently came into contact with the wounded Autobot, Bumblebee. Buster and his father, Sparkplug Witwicky, managed to save Bumblebee's life, and hearing of the Autobots' vital need for fuel, agreed to help them by calling on Sparkplug's mechanical expertise to create a fuel conversion

method that would enable the Autobots to transform Earth fuel into Transformer fuel.

Learning of this plan, the Decepticons kidnapped Sparkplug and forced him to create the fuel conversion device for them. He was rescued by the Autobot, Gears, and the super-powered human known as Spider-Man, but not before he had given the Decepticons what they sought. Energised by their newfound source of fuel, the Decepticons struck against the weakened Autobots lying defeated at their feet. But Sparkplug had tricked the Decepticons, poisoning their fuel with a corrosive acid. When the acid filtered from their fuel lines into vital neural and muscular systems, it was they who fell in defeat. Only the arrival of Shockwave – accidentally reactivated by an Autobot probe – swung the battle once more in the Decepticons' favour.

Since that time both Buster and his father have continued to play pivotal roles in the lives of both the Autobots and the Decepticons. Following directly on from Shockwave's victory over the Autobots, it was Buster – aided by the Autobot surgeon, Ratchet – who kept the Creation Matrix (the force that gives new Transformers life) safe from the Decepticons and aided in the re-animation of Ratchet's fellow Autobots. Eventually, Buster – using the then mindless Transformer known as Jetfire – was able to free the captive Optimus Prime, thereby allowing him to challenge and defeat Shockwave. Buster returned the Creation Matrix to Prime, but later discovered that the Matrix had left behind a message in Buster's mind that told of the Special Teams, combining Transformers that would eventually form the future of Autobot and Decepticon alike.

While Optimus Prime was Shockwave's prisoner, the Autobots forged an alliance with another human – G.B. Blackrock – who had lost both an oil drilling platform and an aerospace plant to the Decepticons. Conversely, both the Autobots and the Decepticons made a common enemy in Josie Beller, a one-time employee of Blackrock's who was almost totally paralysed when Shockwave seized control of the oil drilling platform. She coated her body in micro-

circuitry and returned to hunt Transformers as Circuit Breaker.

The most recent human to come into direct contact with the Transformers is Donny Finkleberg, who was employed by the U.S. Government agency known as Triple-I to impersonate his own comic-book creation called Robot-Master, in an effort to allay the public's concern over giant robots by claiming that they were the tools of a terrorist group headed by Robot-Master himself. Robot-Master was captured by Megatron, who plans to use this deception for his own ends.

'500,000 volts and rising. Transmission circuits ready,' the computer registered subliminally. . .

Question: What happened to the Dinobots?
Answer: In order to battle against Megatron, Ratchet travelled to the Savage Land, located and revived the Dinobots. With their aid, he managed to defeat Megatron, knocking him over the edge of a high cliff. The Dinobots accompanied Ratchet back to the Ark and helped combat the rogue Autobot battle-droid, Guardian. However, the resolution of that battle left Swoop missing, presumed destroyed. The other Dinobots, disgruntled with their Autobot colleagues, left the Ark and headed North. A short while after this, a fault developed in the Dinobots' minds and they reverted to their basic primal state, splitting up and running amok all over the West Coast states of America. At the same time, Swoop had been discovered by a human called Professor Morris who, through his mind control device, made Swoop attack the Autobots. Swoop was rescued, but soon succumbed to the same mental disease as his fellow Dinobots. Optimus Prime and the Autobots took it upon themselves to round up the other four errant Dinobots. Decepticon involvement in their efforts left Prime with many seriously injured Autobots and five comatose Dinobots.

'750,000 volts and rising'. The computer began to create a circuit connecting its power source directly to the keyboard of Adam Reynolds.

Question: Did Shockwave create any new Decepticons while Optimus Prime was his prisoner?

Answer: Yes. Though Prime had managed to transfer the main part of the Creation Matrix's power to Buster Witwicky, enough remained in his mind for Shockwave to give life to his six new creations – Scrapper, Scavenger, Bonecrusher, Long Haul, Mixmaster and Hook, collectively known as the Constructicons. These six possessed the ability to combine with each other to form one huge titan – Devastator. However, the creation of these six used up all the Matrix's power left in Prime's mind, and Shockwave was unable to instil life in his next creation – Jetfire. Buster Witwicky, using the Matrix's power, took control of Jetfire and used him to free Prime. When Shockwave had been defeated, Prime used the Matrix to give Jetfire his life. Jetfire was shortly afterwards inaugurated into the ranks of the Autobots.

'Power store at 1,000,000 volts. Circuit complete.' The computer double-checked that the user's keyboard was now live, and prepared to send the current when the next instructions were typed on to it.

Question: Explain the rise and fall/interaction of Megatron and Shockwave.

Answer: When Megatron fell victim to Sparkplug Witwicky's corrosive fuel, Shockwave adjudged that Megatron's leadership was at fault and concluded that the logical course of action was for him to take command of the Decepticons. Megatron disagreed and the two battled. Shockwave emerged victorious and Megatron was given a simple choice – obey or die. Not wishing the latter, Megatron agreed to serve under Shockwave – secretly plotting to destroy the usurper at the first opportunity. His plans were cut short by Ratchet and the Dinobots, and he was left deactivated in a deep snowdrift.

Shockwave was shortly afterwards defeated by Optimus Prime, and sank without trace into a deep swamp. With both leaders missing, Soundwave – the Decepticons' Communications Officer and second-in-command – took control. When Shockwave freed himself from the swamp, Soundwave returned control of the Decepticons to him. When Megatron returned, he and Shockwave fought each other to standstill and agreed to the logic of a temporary joint leadership.

Q&A concludes.

Further instructions?

The computer's impatient whine jolted Adam awake in his seat. Rubbing tired eyes, he wondered at what point he'd fallen asleep. Regarding the mass of printout at his feet he

HEADS UP TROOPS! HERE SHE COMES!

decided enough was enough. He'd already pushed his luck too far getting this much information, it was time to break the link. Stretching, he hunched once more over the console. He typed the word 'disconnect' and reached for the enter button . . .

Adam paused. With a sigh he realised that once he'd pressed the enter button that was it. Finished, kaput. He'd never be able to access the Decepticon mainframe again. His finger hovered indecisively over the keyboard.

The computer waited.

With a shrug, Adam punched his finger down towards the button, relishing the unnecessary force as contact was made . . .

Adam screamed!

The black shape seemed to come from nowhere, landing squarely on his lap. As he screamed his fright, his convulsive jerk sent both him, his cat – Ulysses, and the chair flying backwards in a spectacular tangle. As if to punctuate the chaos, Adam's computer exploded – the blast spraying shards of metal and plastic outwards with great force. Curled into a ball, cradling the terrified cat within a protective cocoon, Adam waited until the rain of debris was over before looking up at the charred spot that marked where his computer had once stood.

Oblivious to his brush with death and the anguished squeals of his parents as they flew into the room, Adam stared with brimming eyes at the smouldering, blackened pages of his computer printout. No one would believe him now, he realised. The secrets of the Transformers were lost forever. NO – not lost, *he* knew . . . and that was enough. For now, anyway. He wondered if the Autobots had a computer . . .

● **Compiled by Simon Furman**

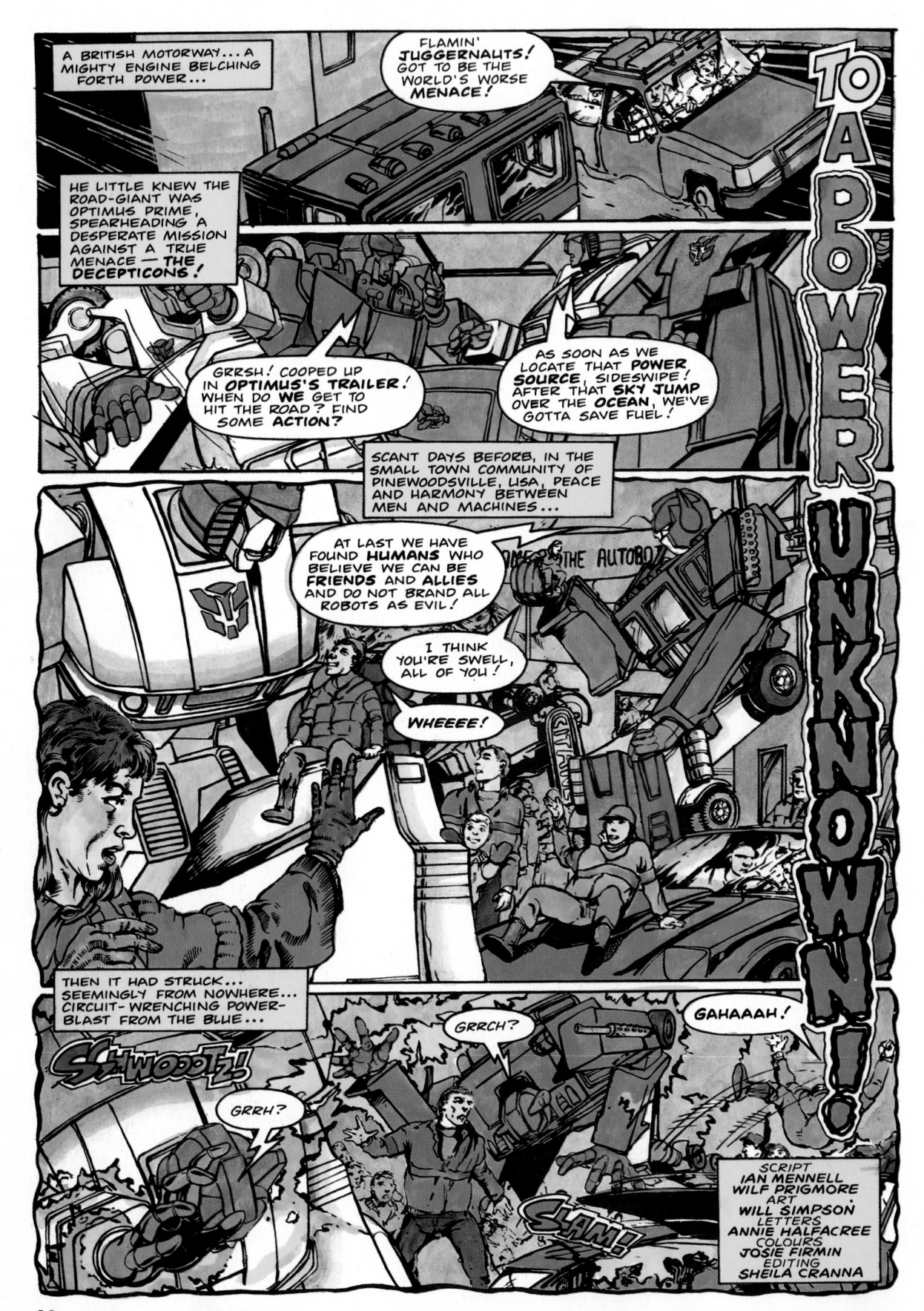

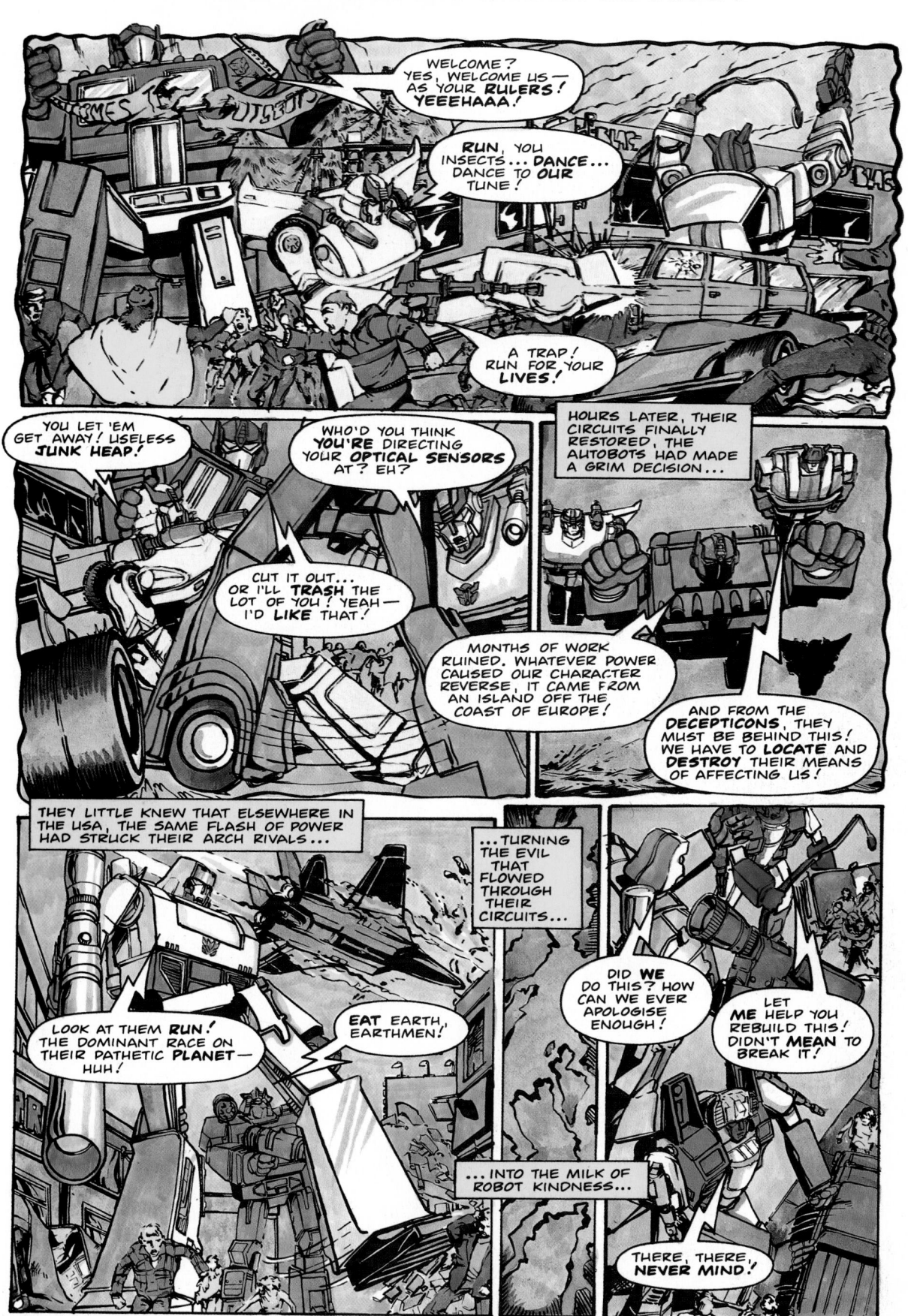

A SIMILAR **POWER-TRACE** HAD LOCATED THE SOURCE OF DISRUPTION AND SOON THE AIR ABOVE THE ATLANTIC RESOUNDED WITH THE ROAR OF JET ENGINES

ALL THIS BICKERING ABOUT WHO SHOULD BE **LEADER**, MEGATRON! WHEN **YOU'RE** OBVIOUSLY THE **RIGHT ROBO** FOR THE JOB!

SO **LIKE** YOU, SHOCKWAVE, TO PLAY YOURSELF DOWN! WHY A **MACHINE** OF YOUR **METAL** DESERVES TO COMMAND!

WE DON'T CONQUER PLANETS WITH **KINDNESS**! THE ACCURSED AUTOBOTS HAVE FOUND A WAY TO REVERSE OUR CIRCUITS. THEY MUST BE STOPPED, **FOLLOW ME**!

I FOLLOW **NO ONE**, MEGATRON! WHEN WE'VE TRASHED OPTIMUS'S LITTLE SCHEME, I'LL BE GUNNING FOR **YOU**!

AND SO, UNBEKNOWN TO EACH OTHER, ENEMY SQUADS OF TRANSFORMERS ARRIVED IN BRITAIN DETERMINED TO FIND AND ERADICATE THE UNKNOWN POWER...

DECEPTICON SWEEP SQUAD. YOU EACH HAVE YOUR CO-ORDINATES! COMPUTER TRACES OPERATIONAL. MAINTAIN CONTACT! SEEK — **DESTROY**!

POWER SOURCE STILL NOT PRECISELY KNOWN. YET I HAVE **OPTIMUS PRIME** IN MY SCANNER, TRANSFORMED... **VULNERABLE**! THIS IS **STARSCREAM** — IN FOR THE KILL!

NOT FAR AWAY IN A SECRET RESEARCH ESTABLISHMENT — A SECRET BRIEFING!

I AM PROFESSOR **PURNEL**, MY ASSISTANT **ZEKE HEILMANN**... AND HERE, READY FOR THE **SECOND** TESTING IS MY **BRAINCHILD**... CODE-NAME **PARD**!

PURNEL'S AUTO-REVERSE DEFENCE SYSTEM... A BREAK-THROUGH IN MODERN WARFARE **IF** IT WORKS!

IT **WILL**, ONCE THE OUTER CIRCUITRY IS PERFECTED! PARD CAN REVERSE COMPUTER-CONTROLLED INSTRUCTIONS TO MISSILES THE WORLD OVER! ANY WEAPONS LAUNCHED AT ALLIED COUNTRIES **RETURNED TO SENDER**!

THE MEREST TOUCH AND THE POWER OF PARD FLOODS THE **ENTIRE** WORLD IN SECONDS! OF COURSE, UNTIL PROPERLY TARGETTED AND PROGRAMMED, IT WILL NOT AFFECT **MAN-MADE** TECHNOLOGY!

THE BLUEPRINT FOR BUILDING THE **HEART** OF PARD! FIVE YEARS OF WATCHING, WAITING SHALL BE REWARDED!

◄ TO A POWER UNKNOWN ►

MAN-MADE PERHAPS... BUT FOR THE ALIEN TECHNOLOGY O, THE BEINGS FROM CYBERTRON, ITS EFFECTS WERE DEVASTATING...

MISSILE TARGETTED AND AWAY... HUH... WHAT... WHAT IS HAPPENING?

STMM!

BWAMF!

ATTACK! AND-AND SOMETHING ELSE... CIRCUITS MALFUNCTIONING!

A SURGE OF POWER! CEREBRAL CIRCUITS JAMMED! IN-BRED CHARACTERISTICS REVERSED!

WHY ARE WE HERE? WHAT DOES IT ALL REALLY MEAN? GIVE PEACE A CHANCE!

DECEPTICON ATTACK! WHY DIDN'T I SENSE IT? WHY DIDN'T THOSE FOOLS IN THE BACK WARN ME?

UMPH! PRIME ALMOST GOT US TRASHED! TIME HE WAS TAKEN OUT! TRANSFORM!

TRANSFORM AND HEAD AFTER PRIME! THAT METAL-HEAD NEEDS RECYCLING!

AUTOBOTS BELOW, VISUAL CONTACT! INSTRUCTIONS TO DESTROY, BUT WHY? NO, WE SHOULD BE FRIENDS... ALLIES!

OFF THE ROAD... A SITTING TRUCK! WIPE-OUT TIME!

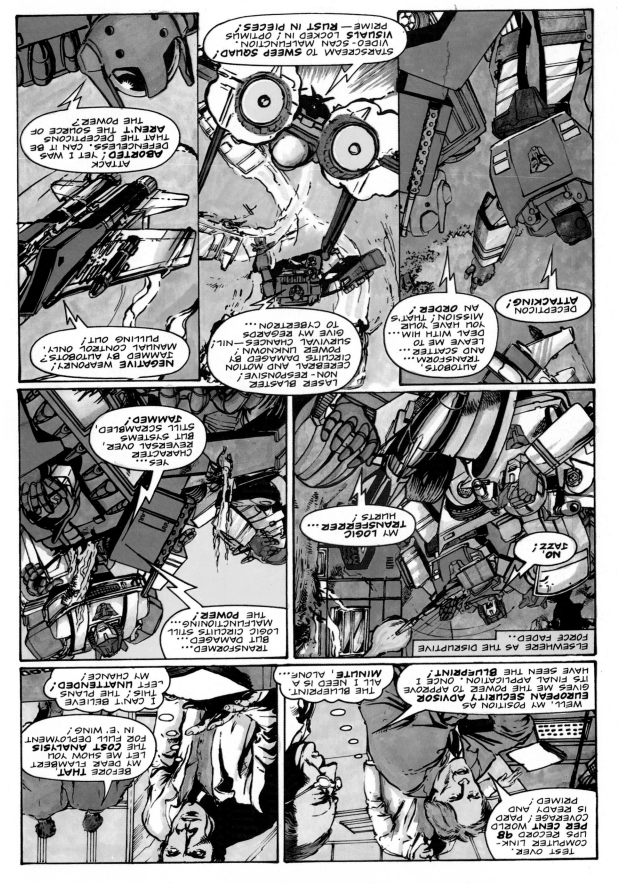

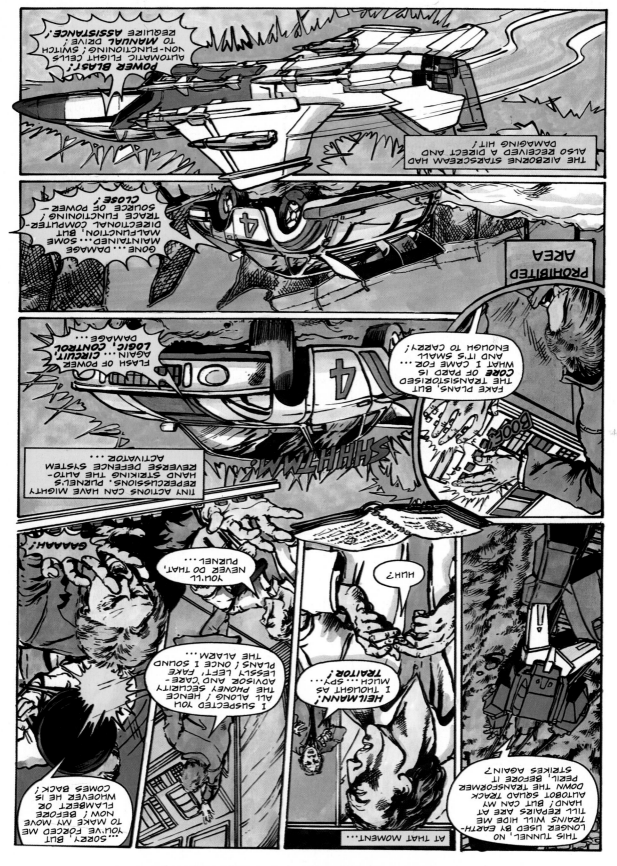

◄ TO A POWER UNKNOWN ►

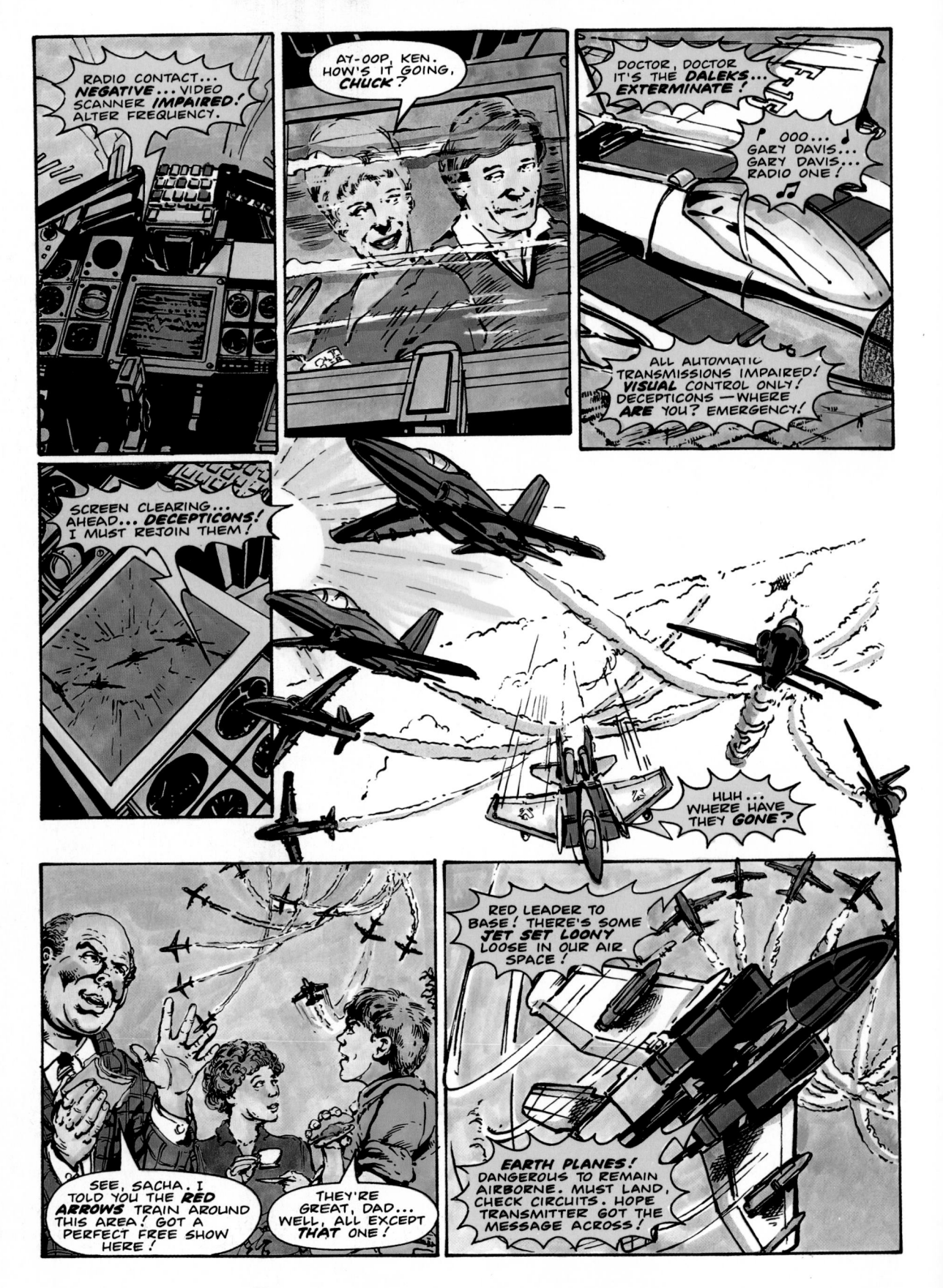

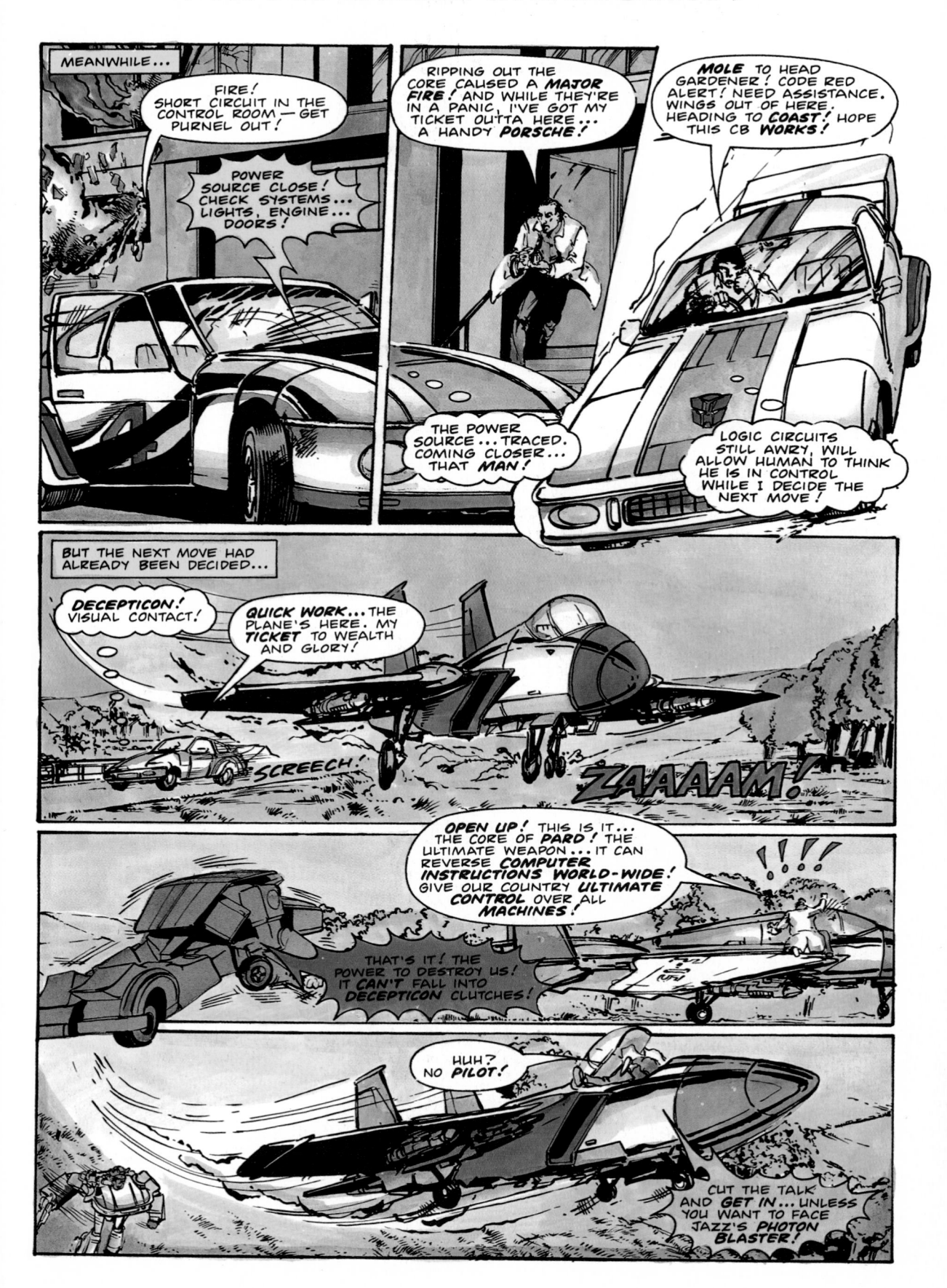

◀ TO A POWER UNKNOWN ▶

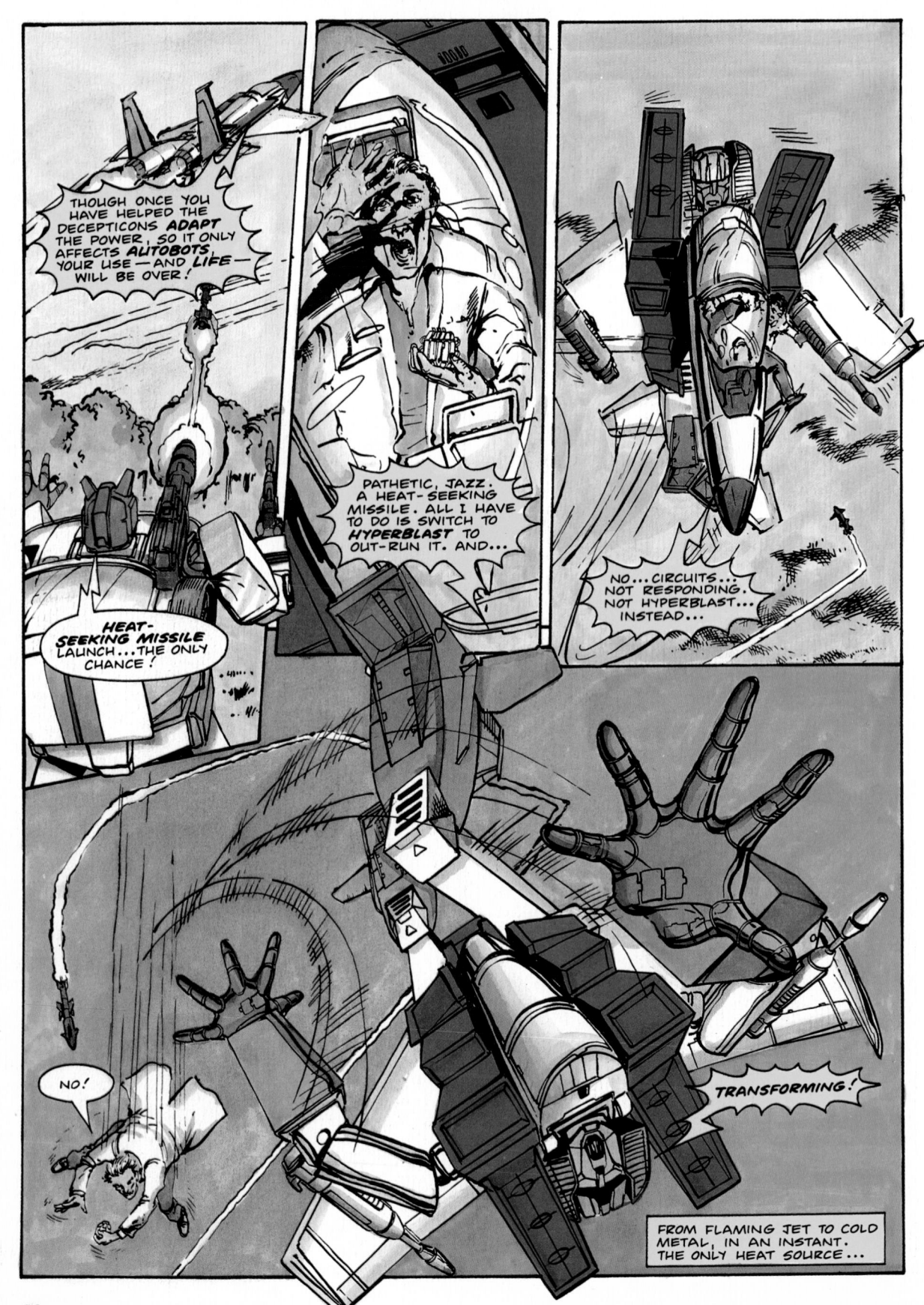

THOUGH ONCE YOU HAVE HELPED THE DECEPTICONS *ADAPT* THE POWER, SO IT ONLY AFFECTS *AUTOBOTS* YOUR USE — AND *LIFE* — WILL BE OVER!

HEAT-SEEKING MISSILE LAUNCH...THE ONLY CHANCE!

PATHETIC, JAZZ. A HEAT-SEEKING MISSILE. ALL I HAVE TO DO IS SWITCH TO *HYPERBLAST* TO OUT-RUN IT. AND...

NO...CIRCUITS... NOT RESPONDING. NOT HYPERBLAST... INSTEAD...

NO!

TRANSFORMING!

FROM FLAMING JET TO COLD METAL, IN AN INSTANT. THE ONLY HEAT SOURCE...

◄ TO A POWER UNKNOWN ►

REPEATED SWEEPS OVER THE AREA HAVE REVEALED NOTHING BEYOND A SERIOUS *FIRE* AT THE RESEARCH CENTRE!

SKULKING, HIDING! THIS IS *NOT* THE DECEPTICON WAY, BUT UNTIL WE HAVE OUR *FUEL SUPPLY* AND HAVE *CONQUERED* THE AUTOBOTS, SO BE IT!

SEARCH COMPLETE. BACK TO BASE!

ALREADY MY CIRCUITS ARE *REPAIRING* THEMSELVES. CONTACT WITH OTHER *AUTOBOTS* ESTABLISHED. ONLY *OPTIMUS PRIME* HIMSELF REQUIRES ASSISTANCE!

AND SO...

WHAT'S THAT UP AHEAD? MODERN SCULPTURE? STILL LIFE? *ART*, THEY CALL IT...

...*RUBBISH* I CALL IT! *HUUUH?*

JAZZ TO *RATCHET*, UK BASE! OUR AUTOMATIC SYSTEMS ARE *GO!* BUT WE'VE GOT A PATIENT FOR YOU!

THE END.

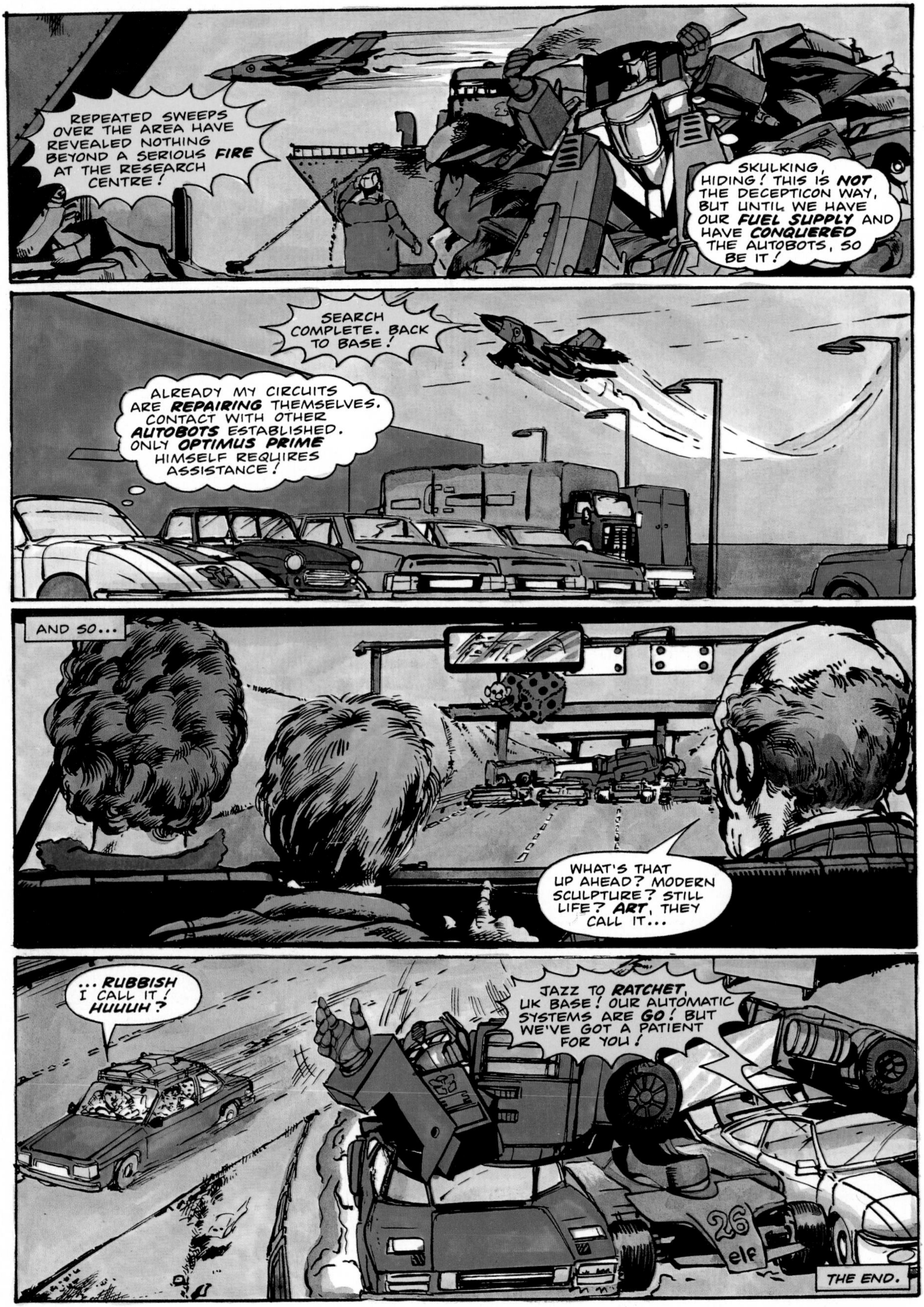

OPTIMUS PRIME

DATAFILE – meaning?

Decepticon mainframe computer records log.

Elaborate.

History/profile of each Decepticon/Autobot currently on war-status, both on Earth and Cybertron. Do you require standard sample?

Yes.

Sample DATAFILE ready for high-speed pulse transmission. Printout?

Yes.

Running. . .

OPTIMUS PRIME: Current Autobot leader (inaugurated 1st Cycle 820, Cybertron-time). Abandoning plans to train in his chosen capacity of Medical officer, Optimus Prime enrolled in the Autobot army as soon as the Decepticons declared war. His capacity for fast, decisive action and the inate ability to inspire respect and obedience in others marked him immediately as officer material. His first command put him in control of the Elite Flying Corps, the Autobots' airborne forces, and soon after he was made field Commander of the entire Autobot army. But with overall control of the army remaining with the Council Of Autobot Elders, he soon found that his hands were tied when it came to making any positive strikes against the advancing Decepticons.

Unknown to the Council, Prime began to sanction unauthorised strategies, and when at last Emirate Xaaron persuaded High Councillor Traachon to surrender complete control of the army to him, he was able to make the first positive counter-strike against the Decepticons, halting Megatron's advance into Iacon. With the largest Autobot city-state safe against the Decepticons, it became the base of the Autobot resistance. Heartened by this victory, Autobots in other city-states began to repel Decepticon assaults with renewed vigour.

The war continued for a further thousand years (Earth-time) until Autobot scientists discovered that Cybertron – shaken loose from its orbit and sent hurtling through space – was heading towards a huge asteroid belt, large enough to destroy it. The Autobots built a vast spacecraft – dubbed The Ark – and Prime, accompanied by a crack troop of Autobots, piloted it into outer space; there to destroy the asteroids. A Decepticon attack on The Ark resulted in a crash-landing on a barren planet.

Four million years later, The Ark's computers re-built and modified the fallen Autobots and Decepticons. Isolated from Cybertron, Prime –

and those other Autobots who had survived – took it upon themselves to foil Megatron's plans for the conquest of this new planet, known as Earth. The war between the Autobots and the Decepticons began anew (albeit on a smaller scale) on Earth, and to this day Prime remains as committed as ever to ending the Decepticon threat, and safeguarding the people of Earth.

OPTIMUS PRIME (SUB-HEAD: ABILITIES/ WEAKNESSES): Optimus Prime possesses the ability to transform from robot mode into the likeness of an Earthen Tractor Trailer, and then to further sub-divide that form into three autonomous components.

His command module is the storehouse of his vast knowledge and strength. He can lift 400,000 lbs and a blow from his fist exerts a force of 12,000 lbs per square inch. He carries a laser rifle. Roller is a small, cart-shaped device which he uses to slip unobtrusively behind enemy lines. He can maintain radio control over it up to a distance of 1,200 miles, and having Roller present somewhere is like being there himself. His Combat Deck is a vast storehouse of weaponry and supplies, both for himself and for his fellow Autobots.

Though Optimus Prime can function as three independent modules, injury to one module is felt by the other two. Also it takes considerable effort to split his consciousness in three different directions and not lose efficiency to some degree. Though the Command Module – Optimus himself – could survive without the other two, they could not survive without him.

DATAFILE sample ends. Further instructions?

Hold.

Holding. . .

The Return of the TRANSFORMERS

**Danny had met the giant robots once before.
Soon he was to get caught up in one of their battles!**

Danny Phillips stared down at the beach. From his vantage point, high on the cliff top, he could see for miles; yet wherever he looked he was greeted with the same sight – far from golden sands littered with rotting seaweed and driftwood, left by the now retreating tide. A brisk sea-breeze buffeted the boy's face, and his clothes, rain-soaked and heavy, clung to his body.

Far to Danny's left and set back from the beach, lay the hotel that he and his mother had checked in to at the start of their vacation a week earlier. Although it now occurred to Danny, standing on this dismal windswept outcrop, that 'vacation' wasn't really the word to use.

What had his mother called their trip? 'A get-away-from-it-all break'? Yes, that was it . . . Jennifer Phillips had decided she and her son needed time alone to 'work out' their problems and a quiet, restful holiday on the coast in the depths of winter was, apparently, just what was wanted.

Wearily shaking his head, Danny began to pick his way down the gently ·sloping cliff face. He knew only too well when things had started to go wrong between him and his mother. It had been last summer . . .

Throughout the months leading to September, New York's popular press claimed that giant shape-changing robots had been sighted in the state of Oregon and other parts of the country. Most of the stories were vague and speculative, but the general opinion seemed to be that the creatures were extra-terrestrial in origin, and their savage assaults on installations, both civilian and military, suggested they were far from benevolent.

Like many others his age, Danny had avidly followed the reports, yet he was convinced that if the robots were aliens – which he really believed – then they were from a civilization so advanced as to have long ago renounced violence. Indeed, Danny had come to the conclusion that the robots had visited earth to promote peace and understanding, and their purpose had been misinterpreted by the authorities. And after all, he'd had first-hand experience . . .

Caught in a bank bombed by desperate thieves, he had been rescued by a group of the giant robots. The creatures disguised as, amongst other vehicles, fire and tow trucks, had slipped away quietly; but once passed healthy and discharged from hospital, Danny began a frantic search for the miraculous beings that had saved his life. He diligently collected as many news clippings on the robots as possible, filling scrapbook after scrapbook, yet he was unable to find any clue to where the Transformers, as some newspapers called the robots, might possibly appear next.

FRIENDLESS

It was when Danny's school work started to suffer that his mother became anxious.

"Your grades are slipping," she'd murmured at the breakfast table one morning. Just a simple, "Your grades are slipping," except Danny knew she'd never leave it at that. No, she just had to tell him how his obsession (as she called his interest in the robots) was

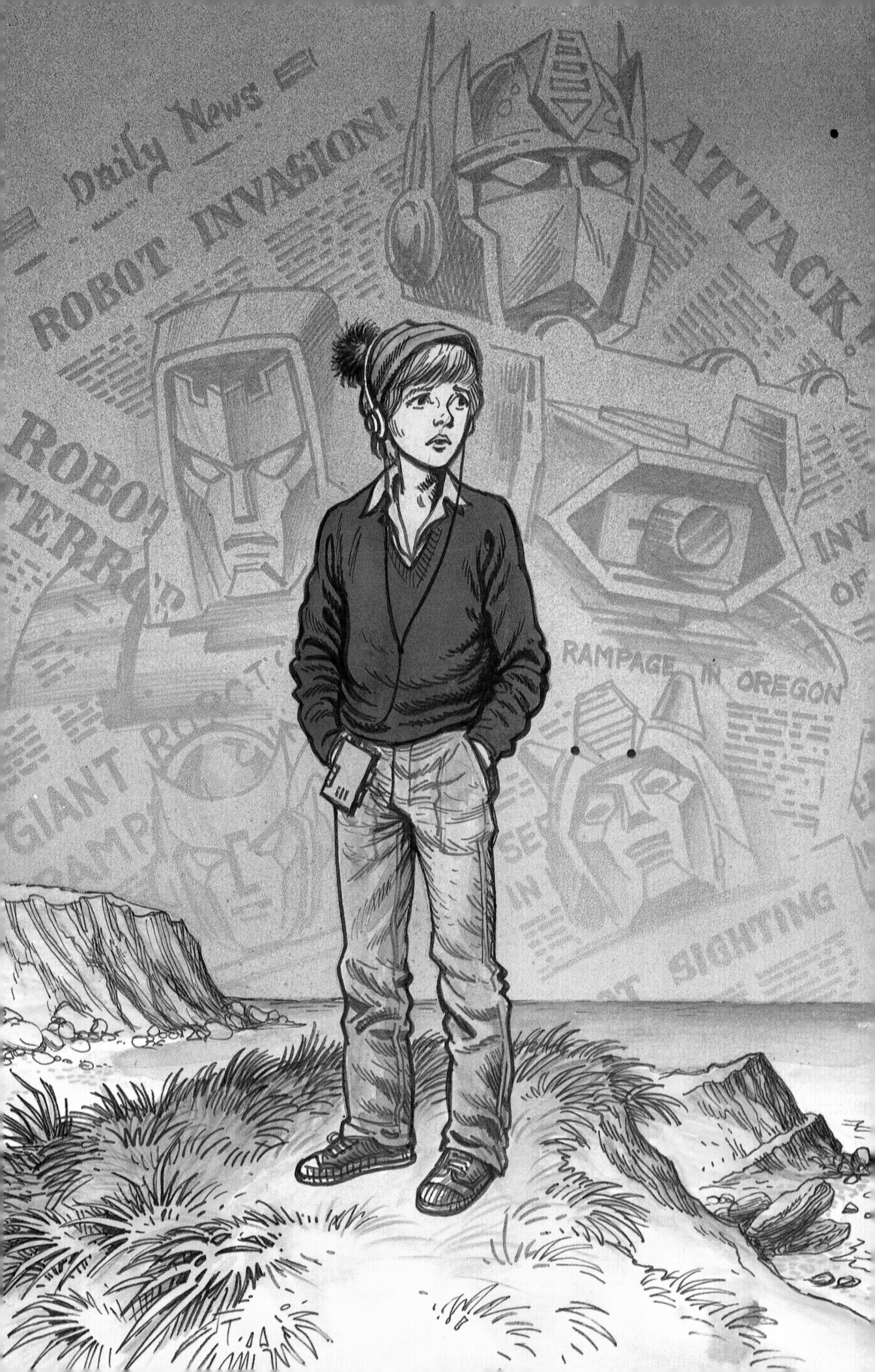

unhealthy. She had to remind him how he'd not seen any of his friends in weeks. How he –

The rest had fallen on deaf ears. Danny rose slowly from his place at the table and silently left the kitchen.

That had been the first, but far from the last occasion, on which Jennifer Phillips had broached the subject; and as he made his way towards the beach, his Nikes running shoes caked in mud, Danny wondered guiltily whether perhaps his mother had been justified in her concern. It was true he'd stopped seeing his friends . . . although it hadn't been completely up to him. The other kids had begun to avoid him and, if they met even by chance, they teased and mocked him over his interest in the robots. They just didn't seem to understand and seeing no reason as to why he should make them understand, Danny kept very much to himself.

And his grades? Had his grades slipped? Until now Danny believed they hadn't, at least not noticeably . . . Besides, even if they had, he was still an above average student. Grades were no longer important. All that mattered was finding the robots.

However grades *were* important, at least to his mother and after much badgering and threatening, she'd finally arranged to take Danny out of school and booked the pair of them into the Chalton, or Carlton, or whatever the hotel was called. Danny needed a complete break from the city. Given enough time, his mother said, he'd begin to forget about the robots, and she wanted to help him do just that.

THE POWER PLANT

The only problem was, their hastily planned trip happened to coincide with what Danny believed to be the worst weather in over twenty years. With few residents and seemingly fewer staff, The Charlton appeared practically deserted, as did the surrounding area. Shops and amusement arcades were closed for the winter, and would, no doubt, remain boarded up and shuttered for many bitterly cold months. The only thing to offer even the slightest interest to Danny was a power plant, situated some miles down the coast from the Charlton hotel.

"It's a government installation designed to investigate the possibilities of converting 'wave power' into electricity," Simpson, a janitor at the Charlton, had told Danny, while discussing the power station soon after they'd arrived. Yet even this had failed to capture the boy's imagination and up till now he'd steered clear of the plant, preferring to spend his days wandering up and down the beach, lost in thought. He was doing his best to forget the Transformers, but they were more on his mind than ever. Also, unbeknown to his mother, he'd brought his Transformers scrapbook, which was hidden in his bag back at the hotel . . .

"Danny . . . It's nearly time for lunch. Danny!" It was his mother. She was searching for him, and immediately deciding that even an afternoon exploring the power station was preferable to yet another meal in the hotel's chilly and almost empty restaurant, Danny jumped the remaining distance to the beach and began to jog along the still moist sands.

DANGEROUS FLAWS

Deep within Mount St. Hilary and deeper still within a crippled, seemingly dead starship, Optimus Prime's metallic fingers flowed across the keyboard, as he expertly searched the Ark's computer banks:

REQUIRED DATA ON:–
THE AERIALBOTS

Responding to this unspoken command, a large video screen flickered into emerald life:–

DATAFILE:
THE SPECIAL TEAMS
CLASSIFICATION:
THE AERIALBOTS
SUB-CLASSIFICATIONS:
SILVERBOLT – COMMANDER
SKYDIVE – STRATEGIST
FIREFLIGHT –
RECONNAISANCE
SLINGSHOT – GROUND
TROOPS SUPPORT
AIR RAID – WARRIOR
NOTE:
FIVE AERIALBOTS COMBINE TO
FORM AIR
WARRIOR SUPERION
FURTHER INFORMATION KEY:
1250

Haunted by words spoken months earlier, Prime left the computer terminal and moved towards his command chair.

"I will not allow the Creation Matrix to be perverted," he had said and at the time, despite the urging of some of his fellow Autobots, he had been adamant. The Matrix would not be used to create, as Prowl had so vocally suggested, a new generation of 'Ultimate Autobots', designed specifically for combat.

No . . . such a move would only have caused an unprecedented escalation in the Autobot/Decepticon conflict. Undoubtedly reducing the Earth to a battle-scarred husk, much like their home planet, Cybertron.

But . . . things had changed. Megatron had returned to lead the Decepticons and the war had surprisingly turned against the Autobots. So in a desperate but necessary measure to counter his enemies' air superiority, Prime had reversed his previous decision and overseen the manufacture of the Aerialbots.

Then, using the Matrix, the sacred means of Autobot generation, he had imbued their cold, metallic shells with life. Yet like so many other creations, the Aerialbots were flawed; each had his own weakness, and as he slumped into the command chair, Prime considered that perhaps these weaknesses

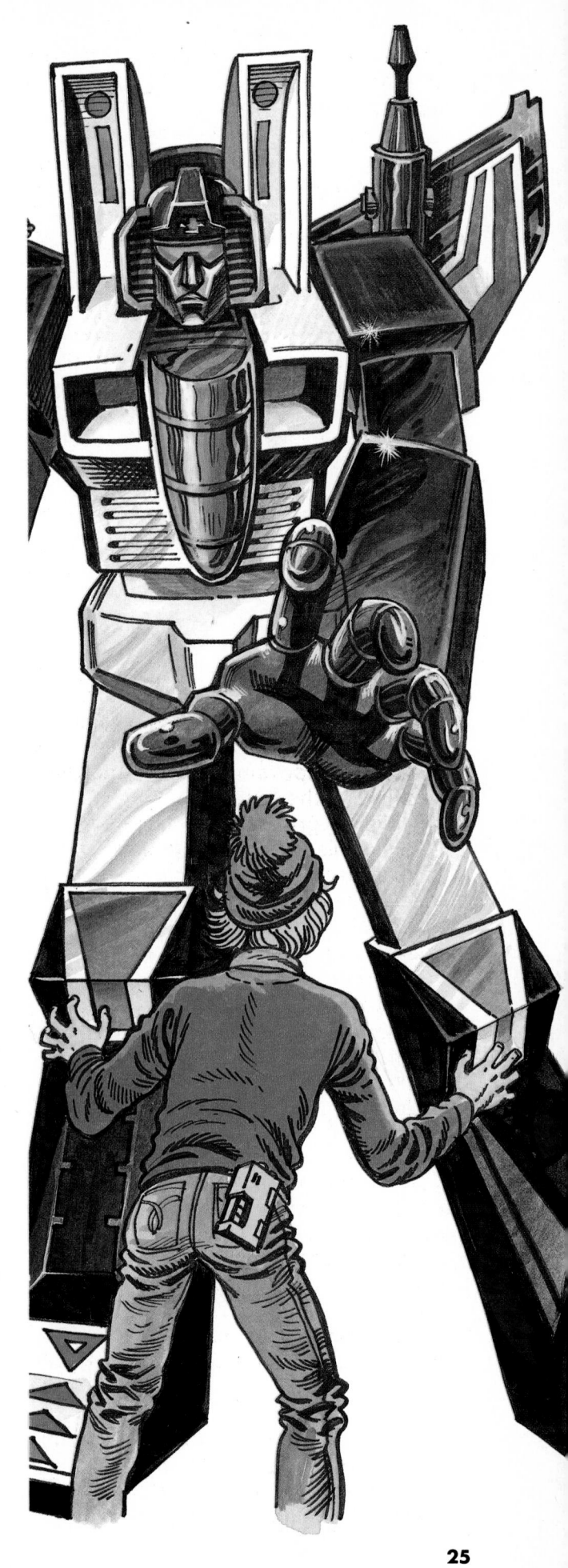

far outweighed the Aerialbots' effectiveness as Autobot warriors.

MISSION FOR JETFIRE

"Prime? You asked to see me?" Optimus looked up to see the sleek form of the renegade Decepticon, Jetfire, enter his private chambers.

"Yes, Decepticon agents have been sighted close to a small town on the East Coast. I'd like you to take command of the Aerialbots and travel there to investigate. Trailbreaker will inform you of the precise co-ordinates."

"Very well." Jetfire turned and made as if to leave.

"Wait, Jetfire!" Prime called him back. "Wait . . . I'd like you to review the program the computer's currently running. It concerns the Aerialbots . . . outlines their individual weaknesses, their personal phobias. Needless-to-say, the information is of an extremely confidential nature, but I'd like you to use it, and the opportunity provided by this mission to test the Aerialbots' responses in an actual combat situation. You're to undermine their decisions, force them into conflict with one another. By the mission's end, I'd like to know whether or not they're worthy of the name Autobot."

Jetfire, the Aerialbots flying beside him, banked over the Cascades mountain range and headed eastward. Prime's briefing had made little sense. After first refusing to use the Matrix in the fight against Megatron, he had surprised everyone by ordering the creation of the Special Teams. Surely he didn't now regret that decision? Perhaps . . . but it wasn't Jetfire's place to question his commander, or the mission he had been entrusted with . . . no matter how unpopular that made him.

"I thought you led the Aerialbots, Silverbolt," Skydive muttered, seemingly careless of the fact that he was well within Jetfire's audio range.

"Yes," agreed Air Raid, "since when has an ex-Decepticon been placed in command of such an important mission?"

Remaining uncharacteristically silent, Silverbolt offered his companions no opinion as to why the leadership of their group had been placed in Jetfire's

hands. Yet as he climbed higher and higher, fear gripping his circuits, the Aerialbot decided he knew why . . . it was because of his vertigo. Vertigo, that even now screamed at him to stop, and fly towards the safety of solid ground. Vertigo, that would obviously in Prime's opinion affect Silverbolt's ability to lead.

TRANSFORMERS AT LAST!

Danny passed the empty gatehouse, strolled across the lifeless fore-court and entered what he assumed to be the power station's main building. Why the plant was completely deserted, he couldn't even guess at. Perhaps today was a local holiday. He didn't know and he didn't care. He'd been offered the perfect opportunity for a little exploration and he'd seized it with both hands.

At first Danny thought the muffled hum was part of his day-dream. Hours of roaming throughout the plant had finally convinced him he was alone. Alone to wander in his own world. A world free from problems and misunderstandings. A world that was brutally shattered as the characteristic clatter of working machinery assaulted him from the near-by generator room.

His instincts were to run, to flee, to escape the security guard who undoubtedly lay in wait for him. But he didn't run. Instead, he turned the corner – totally unprepared for the sight that greeted him.

Bent low over a highly polished metallic contraption, Danny could see three unearthly figures . . . Immensely tall figures painted in silver, shades of colour and black. Robotic figures! He'd found them! After months of patient waiting, Danny had at last found the Transformers. Found them here, where he'd least expected to see them.

He ran forward, and then abruptly stopped. Stacked in the corner of the cavernous room were countless glowing cubes of an enormous size. And to the right of these, there was what could only be described as a cage of brightly shimmering energy. Inside this, reminding Danny of captured animals, were trapped the missing power plant workers.

Danny bit his lower lip, the way he did in class when asked a difficult

question. Why would these robots, who were obviously of the same race as those who had pulled him from the burning bank during the raid, want to hold factory workers captive? For that matter, what were they doing in a government power station? He was confused, and suddenly all his theories about the robots no longer made sense.

THE ENEMY LOCATED!

The Aerialbots circled above the small cluster of buildings. They'd travelled the distance from the Ark at an incredible speed and now, according to Air Raid's sensors, their Decepticon quarry lay directly below.

"That's a power plant of some kind; the Decepticons must be using a power siphon to convert electricity into Energon cubes with which to fuel themselves," Jetfire asserted. "Skydive, perhaps you could suggest possible battle tactics."

"Er . . . well," the Aerialbot strategist stuttered. "Perhaps it's advisable for one of us to land and determine our enemies' exact strength, before we commit ourselves to any particular action."

"Nonsense," Jetfire retorted, "such a move may alert the Decepticons to our presence. A surprise assault is what's needed."

"Oh . . . perhaps you're right," Skydive agreed meekly.

"No . . . no he's not!" cried Fireflight.

"Well I agree with Jetfire," Slingshot shouted, suddenly speeding groundward. Being weakest of the Aerialbots, he was resented by his comrades. Perhaps now with Jetfire's new leadership, he'd be able to impress upon them his usefulness.

"Typical," Silverbolt said. "We'd best follow. He won't stand a chance against the Decepticons alone!"

Inside the power plant, Danny squirmed to be free from the huge hand that was forcing the air from his lungs. This wasn't the way things were supposed to be! No matter what the Press said, the robots weren't supposed to behave this way. They *weren't*. As the pain round his ribs increased and his vision began to blur, the outer wall seemed to buckle – and then it suddenly shattered, as a second group of Transformers forced their way into the power plant.

"Jetfire!" Danny's captor sneered, dropping the boy to the ground.

SAVED!

Danny scambled to his feet, rubbing his head. He'd momentarily lost consciousness and now he saw that the workmen had been freed and the seemingly rival robotic factions were locked in deadly combat.

"Stay right where you are, Skywarp!" Danny heard a robot cry, firing a strange hand-held weapon at an opponent. But the opponent mysteriously vanished and a beam of bright light struck instead the store of glowing cubes Danny had seen earlier.

"Fireflight!" Jetfire shouted across the generator room, "Skydive's megablast has struck the energon cubes. Their molecular bonds are starting to break down. They could explode any second! You take the boy and fly to safety."

"No, I can't!" Fireflight protested. "You know I'm the most hazardous flier. You know –"

"Don't argue. There's little time!"

Danny was suddenly swept up in Fireflight's hand and then the hand was gone, and the boy found himself strapped into the cockpit of a Phantom jet, speeding incredibly fast away from the exploding power station. Despite the safety harness, Danny was rocked this way and that; the cockpit began to rattle and his head throb. And then finally as darkness started to overtake him, he could see the Charlton. Standing on the beach outside the hotel was his mother and the members of staff. He felt the robotic craft come into land and then he was lifted down to join her and held tightly in his mother's grasp as she screamed up at the Aerialbot to leave her son alone, go away and just leave him alone!

Fireflight wanted to explain. Wanted to tell the distraught humans how poor a flier he was … how the boy wasn't really injured. How he was only dazed and would soon be recovered, but it seemed pointless. They wouldn't listen, they never did. Instead, the Aerialbot turned his attention to his companions, who were landing on the beach about him.

"Where are Jetfire and Silverbolt?" he asked Air Raid.

"I'm not sure. The Decepticons used the confusion caused by the explosion to sneak back to their fortress. I think our two leaders have gone after Starscream…"

UNDER ATTACK!

Silverbolt flew along side Jetfire, all the time battling with his vertigo. A short distance ahead of them sped Starscream and the Aerialbot was determined that it would be he who captured the Decepticon and not the upstart who had usurped his authority.

Suddenly Starscream turned, launching twin missiles at the pair of Autobots. Both struck Jetfire and he fell, spiralling, to the ocean. It was useless … Starscream was well out of Silverbolt's range and heading back towards the power plant before the Aerialbot's sensors registered what had happened. There was only one course of action left!

"Aerialbots – Combine!" Silverbolt shouted back to his comrades on the beach and within seconds, the Aerialbots were airborne, combining to form the single-minded, incredibly mighty Autobot known as Superion.

Superion caught Starscream with ease and grasped hold of his tail wing, violently throwing him towards the ground. Slate and timbers splintered as the Decepticon crashed into The Charlton. Wasting little time in following his initial assault, Superion landed beside what remained of the hotel and began to sift through the wreckage in the hope of uncovering his now buried prey.

"Stop!" Danny cried, as he ran towards the robot. "Can't you see the destruction you're causing? And for what? So you can continue fighting? It's pointless … just pointless!"

Superion struggled, but failed to understand the small human's words. It was confusing and unproductive to try to assimilate the conflicting personalities of his constituent identities and so by necessity his thought processes were primitive. He had a single purpose — the destruction of the Decepticons, and seeing that Starscream had used this lull in the battle to escape, he slowly turned and waded into the ocean, intending to retrieve the stricken Jetfire and return to the Ark.

AFTER THE BATTLE . . .

The door to Prime's chambers glided shut behind Jetfire. The Autobot leader had been informed of the Aerialbot's performance . . . told of how Silverbolt valiantly fought against his vertigo; how the group supported one another. But he didn't know of the resentment felt towards Slingshot, didn't know how Fireflight's poor flying was not only a danger to passengers but to himself. And perhaps more importantly, Jetfire had not told Prime of how inadequate Superion was in situations other than combat. No, these were problems the Aerialbots must solve themselves, without the interference of Jetfire and Optimus Prime.

Danny Phillips stared down at the ocean. He'd been wrong about the robots; they were not the miraculous beings he'd thought them to be. They fought and squabbled like humans and as his mother parked their rented car behind him on the shore road, Danny took out from under his arm the now battered scrap book he'd retrieved from the demolished Charlton Hotel.

"Danny, it's time to leave," he heard his mother call.

"Coming!" Danny replied, tossing the book into the water.

And as mother and son began the long drive home, the scrapbook floated slowly out to sea . . .

By James Hill

The Transformers

? QUESTIONS ?

Reckon you know quite a bit about our resident robots in disguise, eh? Well, here's your chance to prove it. We've scoured the Transformers story so far, microscopically examined the ranks of the heroic Autobots, and taken an in-depth look at those evil Decepticons, to come up with a quiz that'll tax the most ardent Transformers fan to his or her limits. So you can tell just how high your Transformers IQ is, we've a system of scoring for you to follow. Read the instructions and then off you go. . .

HOW TO THREEPLAY.

Each of the questions is made up of three parts. The first of each set is the easiest, the last the hardest. Each set has a specific theme. A correct answer to part one scores 10 points and means you can move on to part two of the question. If you correctly answer part two you receive a *further* 20 points and move on to part three. Three correct answers means you scoop the maximum points for that particular question – 60 points *in total*. If you fail to answer part two or three of a particular question, your score is either 10 points or 30 points, depending on how far you got. You must answer the parts in sequence; if you cannot answer parts one or two, you must move on to the next question. You'll find the answers and your overall score rating on page 32. No peeking now!

QUESTION A:
Part 1 (score 10 points for a correct answer) – Which Decepticon Commander were the Dinobots created to battle, following the Ark's crash-landing on Earth?

Check your answer and move on to part two if correct.

Part 2 (score a further 20 points for a correct answer) – One of the Dinobots transforms into a likeness of the dinosaur known as Tyrannosaurus rex. Is it Grimlock, Sludge or Swoop?

Check your answer and move on to part three if correct.

Part 3 (score a further 30 points for a correct answer) – Which Autobot freed the Dinobots from the tar-pit in which they lay imprisoned for four million years?

QUESTION B:
Part 1 (score 10 points for a correct answer) – Why did Megatron find it necessary to kidnap the human, Sparkplug Witwicky?

Check your answer and move on to part two if correct.

Part 2 (score a further 20 points for a correct answer) – Which costumed super-hero was instrumental in freeing Sparkplug from the Decepticons' stronghold?

Check your answer and move on to part three if correct

Part 3 Though Sparkplug supplied the Decepticons with what they required, he outwitted them. How?

QUESTION C:
Part 1: (score 10 points for a correct answer) – The Autobots' giant spacecraft – The Ark – was created to avert a danger that threatened from space. What was that danger?

Check your answer and move on to part two if correct.

Part 2: (score a further 20 points for a correct answer) – Who pressed the fateful button that sent the Ark hurtling towards Earth?

Check your answer and move on to part three if correct.

Part 3 (score a further 30 points for a correct answer) – Into which dormant volcano in Oregon did the Ark crash?

QUESTION D:
Part 1 (score 10 points for a correct answer) – Study illustration D. What is the name given to the battle droid on the receiving end of some rough treatment from Snarl?

Check your answer and move on to part 2 if correct.

Part 2 (score a further 20 points for a correct answer) – When he first appeared, he was under the control of the Ark's living computer. What was that computer affectionately known as?

Check your answer and move on to part 3 if correct.

hreeplay Quiz!

[F]

Part 3 (score a further 30 points for a correct answer) – Which Dinobot was responsible for his eventual destruction – and almost ended up being destroyed at the same time?

QUESTION E:
Part 1 (score 10 points for a correct answer) – Which Autobot was originally created as a Decepticon?

Check your answer and move on to part two if correct.

Part 2 (score a further 20 points for a correct answer) – Name the force used to give Transformers life that Buster Witwicky used to take control of this air-borne Transformer.

Check your answer and move on to part three if correct.

Part 3 (score a further 30 points for a correct answer) – What ceremony saw this Transformer officially become an Autobot?

QUESTION F:
Part 1 (score 10 points for a correct answer) – Bombshell, Kickback and Shrapnel. What collective title describes these three Decepticons?

Check your answer and move on to part two if correct.

Part 2 (score a further 20 points for a correct answer) – Scrapper, Mixmaster, Bonecrusher, Scavenger and Hook. Which Constructicon is missing from the list? See illustration F.

Check your answer and move on to part three if correct.

Part 3 (score a further 30 points for a correct answer) – Sludge, Snarl, Grimlock, Slag, Dirge and Swoop. Which is the odd Transformer out? See illustration F.

QUESTION G:
Part 1 (score 10 points for a correct answer) – Joanie, Jenny or Jessie. Which is the correct name for Buster Witwicky's girlfriend?

Check your answer and move on to part two if correct.

Part 2 (score a further 20 points for a correct answer) – Donny Finkleberg was employed by the government to impersonate his own comic-book creation. What was the name of that creation?

Check your answer and move on to part three if correct.

Part 3 (score a further 30 points for a correct answer) – This millionaire/industrialist befriended the Autobots. What is his name? See Illustration G.

QUESTION H:
Part 1 (score 10 points for a correct answer)– Name the Decepticons' Communications Officer.

Check your answer and move on to part 2 if correct.

Part 2 (score a further 20 points for a correct answer) – Name the five spy cassettes.

Check your answer and move on to part 3 if correct.

Part 3 (score a further 30 points for a correct answer) – There are two sets of twins amongst the spy cassettes. What does the fifth cassette resemble in robot form and what is his name?

Right, that's the lot. Add up your final tally of points and then turn the page to check your rating. ▶

[G]

The Transformers Threeplay Quiz!

! ANSWERS !

Okay, here's how to check your answers as you go through the quiz. The answers are split into three groups – the first of these are the answers to part 1 of each question. A correct answer earns you ten points and the right to move on to part two of the question. The next batch are the answers to part 2 of each question, a correct answer means you gain a further twenty points and move on to part 3. The final batch are the answers to part 3 of each question. If your answers match these, then you add a final thirty points – making your grand total for that question sixty points. When you've marked your answers, add up your total score and see how you fared in our rating chart below.

Part 1 Answers:
Question A – Shockwave. *Question B* – Megatron wanted the fuel conversion formula that Sparkplug was creating for the Autobots, so that his troops would have unlimited fuel. *Question C* – Cybertron found itself heading straight for a huge asteroid belt. *Question D* – Guardian. *Question E* – Jetfire. *Question F* – The Insecticons. *Question G* – Jessie. *Question H* – Soundwave.

Part 2 Answers:
Question A – Grimlock. *Question B* – Spider-Man (he was on the scene in his civilian identity of Peter Parker taking news photographs). *Question C* – Optimus Prime. *Question D* – Aunty. *Question E* – The Creation Matrix (Optimus Prime had transferred its power to Buster's mind for safekeeping). *Question F* – Long Haul. *Question G* – Robot-Master. *Question H* – Frenzy, Rumble, Ravage, Laserbeak, Buzzsaw.

Part 3 Answers:
Question A – Ratchet (who sought out the Dinobots in order to battle Megatron). *Question B* – Sparkplug had added a corrosive acid to the fuel he made for the Decepticons, which eventually burned through into vital circuits. *Question C* – Mount St. Hilary. *Question D* – Swoop. *Question E* – The Rite Of Autobrand. *Question F* – Dirge (he is a Decepticon strike plane, while the others are all Dinobots). *Question G* – G.B. Blackrock. *Question H* – Ravage, who transforms into a likeness of Earth's jaguar.

CHECK YOUR THREEPLAY RATE HERE.

10-150: Hmmm, none too impressive. You're either a relative newcomer to the world of The Transformers or you just haven't been paying attention. Either way, an in-depth read of our *In The Beginning. . .* feature on page 5 is a must.

160-300: Not bad at all, but still a long way off the standard we expect of our readers. Follow the same advice as above.

310-450: Now this is more like it. If you're in the upper reaches of this category, you can consider yourself a bona-fide Transformers expert.

480: A maximum score. Consider yourself amongst the élite of Transformers fans.

MEGATRON

Request access DATAFILE. . .

Access code?

Walther P-38.

Input accepted. DATAFILE open. Key subject designation.

MEGATRON.

Restricted. Security rating?

SH45 – 89.

Cleared. Prepare circuits for high-speed pulse transmission. Printout?

Yes.

Running. . .

MEGATRON: Founder of the DECEPTICON movement (circa 1st Cycle 549, Cybertron-time). He and several like-minded Transformers decided that the Autobot leadership was weak, and the way to power was through chaos and conquest. The nucleus of the new faction – Megatron, Shockwave and Soundwave – went underground, secretly adding to their might in numbers and weaponry. Each new member swore allegiance to the cause of tyranny and terror, exchanging their Autobot badges for the fearsome insignia of the Decepticons.

At first, other Transformers saw the Decepticons as harmless and ignored the serpent that was growing in their midst. By the time concern over these renegade Transformers was given voice, it was too late. Megatron had amassed a mighty army, bent on conquest. As soon as the time was adjudged to be propitious, Megatron and the Decepticons struck – capturing and/or destroying each of the Autobot city-states. A huge web of Decepticon-controlled areas soon formed around the largest city-state (and the seat of the Autobot government) – Iacon. Megatron knew that once Iacon was in their possession, they would control all of Cybertron.

So fierce was the combat, so mighty were the forces unleashed, that Cybertron was shaken loose from its orbit and sent hurtling through space. Megatron decided that once Cybertron was under Decepticon rule, he would transform the entire planet into one vast cosmic dreadnought, with which he would conquer the Universe.

But Megatron's plans were forestalled by the emergence of Optimus Prime as Autobot leader. He melded the remains of his army into a fully effective fighting force and began slowly but surely to halt the Decepticon advance. The war raged on for another thousand years, until both Megatron and Optimus Prime found themselves (together with a number of each's army) deactivated, stranded on a barren planet that would become known to its inhabitants as Earth. Megatron's battle against the Autobots resumed with new vigour when the two factions were revived. Megatron knew that if he could master the boundless energy to be found on Earth, he could return to Cybertron and conquer it once and for all.

When Megatron's schemes almost cost the Decepticons their lives, his command was usurped by his own military operations officer – Shockwave. Since that time – and after a period of rule by Shockwave – the two now co-command the Decepticons. This alliance could be – at best – described as fragile.

MEGATRON (SUB-HEAD: ABILITIES/WEAK-NESSES): Megatron is incredibly powerful and intelligent. His Fusion Cannon can convert any small amount of matter into large quantities of explosive nuclear energy. The Cannon can fire a blast up to twelve miles and release enough energy to flatten a small town. Megatron can use his internal circuitry to connect the Cannon interdimensionally with a black hole in space, where it can draw on anti-matter as its source material. The resultant blast from this energy source is far greater than other discharges, but it creates a tremendous strain on Megatron, with only one blast leaving him considerably weakened.

The only weakness demonstrated thus far by Megatron is a susceptibility to a corrosive fuel. The chemical breakdown of this particular fuel is unknown. Megatron possesses the ability to transform (shrinking as he does so) into a likeness of an Earthen Walther P-38 pistol.

DATAFILE entry ends. More?

No.

Transmission ends. Disconnect. . .

State Games

Out of the ashes of a friendly contest, the Decepticons were born!

"**M**egatron!"

The first blow fractured Sunstreaker's battle mask. Fluid seeped across his forehead and down towards his face.

"Megatron!"

A second blow, this time unseen, splintered the Autobot's shield and almost severed his left arm.

"Megatron!"

Yet another blow and another. Another. A rhythmic assault timed to the crowd's growing chant.

"Megatron! Megatron!"

Sunstreaker took a step backward. He raised his broken arm and with a single graceful movement he cast the now useless mask to the far side of the arena. Fuel and lubricant impaired his vision and the crowd blurred to a deafening roar. Sunstreaker had expected a hard contest; Megatron was a citizen of Tarn, and here in this arena he had the advantage of fighting in front of a home crowd. But something else was wrong. . . terribly wrong.

Gladiatorial contests were common throughout Cybertron. Steeped in tradition, they were primarily designed to test an individual's athletic ability, his aptitude with shield and energy weapon, his acrobatic skill. The actual combat itself was far less important. Yet from the moment of entering the arena, Megatron had fought with an unbelievable ferocity. Every vulgar movement timed to the swaying of his frenzied supporters. Each bestial attack punctuated by their screams. With growing horror, Sunstreaker realized that this was no ritualised conflict he was engaged in. This was. . .

. . .Circuit numbing agony as Megatron's energy axe lodged deep in the golden Autobot's shoulder. The world became dull, the crowd somehow remote and then Sunstreaker was thrown to the arena's smooth surface as with a brutal tug, Megatron tore his weapon free from his opponent's body. Tarn's crowded citizenry howled their approval as their champion loomed towards his stricken foe. He raised the energy axe once more, his pace slow and deliberate. His weapon shimmering in Cybertron's cool night air.

"Megatron! Megatron! Megatron!"

LAST IN A LINE

The Autobot Overlord slowly opened his eyes. His circuits were now fully charged and the growing chant from the arena outside told him he'd soon be presenting another winning gladiator with an award. Electricity hummed and sparked as with weary resignation he pulled away from the circuit-encrusted wall he'd been embedded in.

The fact that his energy levels now needed almost constant replenishing was but another indication of the Overlord's great age. He was last in the line of Autobots that once ruled Cybertron and this fact weighed heavy on him. What had finally caused the planet-wide autocracy of his forefathers to give way to the loose collection of independent states that existed today, the Overlord could not say. But he was convinced that the Autobots' thirst for fuel sources had contributed to the change.

The Overlord himself was testament to the fact that the people of Cybertron were a hardy race. For thousands of years, perhaps longer, natural death had been an alien concept to them; yet with the creation of new Transformer life continuing unabated, it should have come as no surprise that one day the

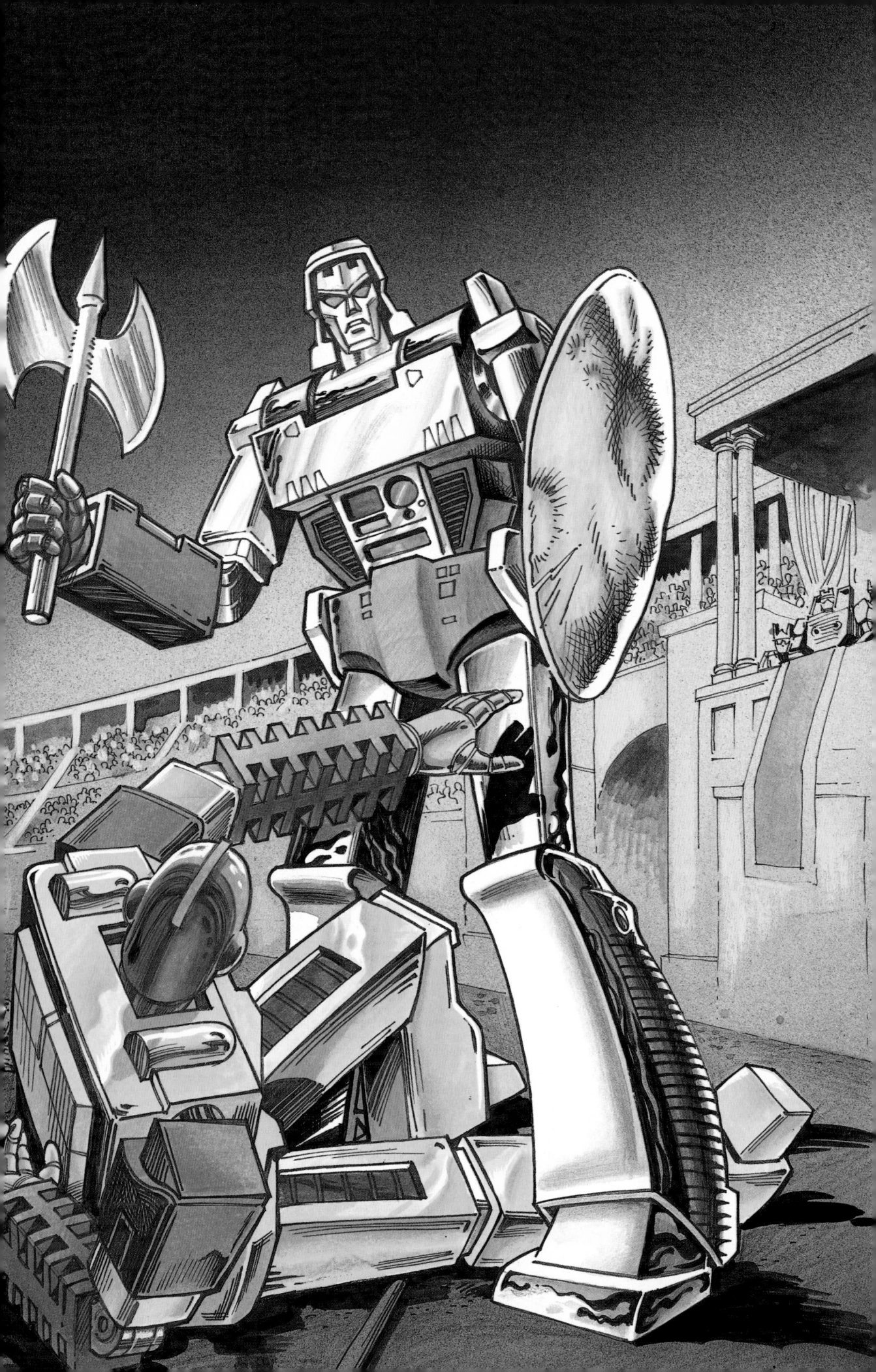

planet would face an unprecedented energy crisis.

That day had arrived. Cities swelled to capacity and competition for fuel had become an intense and bitter struggle. The largest of Cybertron's cities were able to monopolise the planet's meagre resources and as the crisis deepened, not even the Overlord of the time could prevent his people from fragmenting into countless groups. Iacon emerged as the strongest of these newly-created city states and its council of governing elders used their powers to ration and distribute fuel to the city's less advantaged neighbours.

Not so Shockwave, the military ruler of Cybertron's second largest city, Tarn; nor Starscream, figurehead of the controlling dictators of Vos, who used their not inconsiderable fuel stocks to create and maintain vast armies.

"You seem tired." An ebony, cat-like Transformer padded into the cavernous room. He moved with heavy lumbering steps, and pointed fangs, well kept and incredibly long protruded from his mouth as he spoke.

"What? Oh. . . Nightstalker." The Overlord turned with stiffening joints towards his visitor. "No, old friend, at least, no more than usual."

"Then you need much rest." Nightstalker grinned. Along with Ravage, he had been bodyguard to the Overlords for generations and he now thanked the celestial spires that he'd been spared the peculiar melancholy that seemed to take hold of them in the final centuries of their lives. "Do the Games progress well?"

"The Games," the Overlord said, shaking his head slowly, "the games do not progress at all."

He placed an ancient hand on his companion's shoulder. Recent years had seen an alarming increase in tension between the city states. It appeared that now the unthinkable was no longer so and many openly expressed their fears that Cybertron was moving rapidly along a path towards global warfare.

In order to promote good will, the Overlord had used his still considerable influence to organize an inter-state competition. However the Games, as the competition became known, had if anything widened the deadly rift between the city states, particularly Iacon and Tarn. The Overlord rose. "It is time to prepare. . .for the award ceremony," he said, his words punctuated by a long, considered pause.

SOLITARY WATCHER

The spectacle of Gladiatorial combat held little interest for Ravage. He was a creature at home in shadows and the incessant noise of the spectators to such affairs held little appeal to his solitary nature. Yet now he watched, with mounting curiosity as a spectacular drama unfolded in the arena before him. Megatron was indeed a formidable warrior; he fought with a skill and determination Ravage had not seen for centuries.

But there was more to Megatron than combat. His perfectly executed movements suggested the sharp, calculating mind of a true tactician and the manner in which he incited the crowd and bent them to his will, needed a particular spark of leadership Cybertron had not seen since the time of the ruling Overlords. Yes, there was more to Megatron than combat. . . much more.

In the arena, Sunstreaker could no longer hear the crowd. The spectators continued to mock him but there was no sound. There was nothing but an icy grip at the base of the Autobot's neck.

Megatron bent lower, his voice whispered from behind a highly polished battle mask, "It is time this farce ended."

"That is enough!"

The auditorium fell silent and Megatron, shoulders hunched, turned to see a tall, crimson figure. "Prime," he roared, "I'll brook no interference from the likes of you!"

The savage assault took Optimus Prime by surprise, and Iacon's chief athlete found himself lying on the floor of the arena. He tried to regain his footing but Megatron followed his attack through and a gleaming energy axe creased Prime's chest.

Sunstreaker now forgotten, Megatron lurched towards the fallen Iaconian. He raised his energy weapon and. . . his arm fell limply to his side. His eyes widened and he silently stared into the barrel of Prime's photon pistol.

"Put an end to this violence." The

Overlord's voice carried poorly across the arena. He was now dressed in the heavy robes of his office and appeared, to many amongst the crowd, old and feeble.

Prime stood and holstered his weapon. "My Lord, Megatron tried. . ."

"Silence," the Overlord cut in. "You shame these games, but more important, you shame yourselves."

"But. . ."

"Enough, Prime. I shall postpone the award ceremony for another time cycle, and until then, we should all endeavour to re-establish friendly relations."

Ravage rose from his vantage point in the crowd and followed Nightstalker into the tower that housed the Overlord's chambers. Was the Overlord so naive as to be unaware of Megatron's true nature? Perhaps. Perhaps not, it mattered little anyway, for the Overlord would be gone soon and with him the planet's ties to the past. And as he was swallowed by the shadows, Ravage re-

flected that quite possibly, what he had witnessed in the arena this day, was the opening chapter in the bold new history of Cybertron.

SABOTAGE!

Framed by a lightning-streaked sky, Tarn's power plant lay ominously silent. Since the start of the Games, only a minimal workforce had been on duty. Which was unfortunate, for had the full engineering staff been present, the group of saboteurs would undoubtedly have been intercepted long before they located the main generator.

Tornado placed a hand on the generator's cooling system. "It would take little effort," he said, "for me to unleash the power necessary to level this pitiful city. Why do we cloak ourselves in darkness, like common criminals? Why?"

A tall Autobot moved determinedly towards Tornado. His silver coloured body was uncharacteristically free from markings, save for one small insignia and this identified him as a commanding officer in the armed forces of the city state Vos. "We do so because we have been ordered to do so," he said. "And that is all you need to know!"

The officer stepped back and began to lay the explosives the group had brought with them around the base of the generator. The destruction of this power plant was crucial to the future plans of Vos. After such a blatant act of sabotage, Tarn would almost certainly demand retribution and if evidence suggested Iaconian agents. . . the neighbouring cities would soon be at war.

Of course, Vos would maintain a strict neutrality. . . at least until Iacon and Tarn were virtually destroyed, and then, with little effective resistance left to meet them, the armies of Vos would embark on a campaign of global conquest. It was a simple yet effective plan. But it was a plan that failed to account for a solitary Autobot engineer strolling into the generator room.

The engineer stared with horrified fascination at the small group of saboteurs. "By the Primal program," he whispered, all thoughts of his forthcoming work forgotten. "I recognize you – you're members of the athletic team from Vos!"

The engineer turned and began to make for the room's exit. That a group of supposed athletes had infiltrated such an important power station was cause enough for concern, but the engineer had seen the explosives strapped to the generator and even an Autobot of his limited thought processes could guess at the saboteurs' grim intention!

He opened his wrist communicator and began to broadcast a frantic message to the power plant's security officer. Yet this action proved futile as with ease, Tornado used his wind-creating powers to hoist the Autobot aloft and throw him violently against the side of the enormous generator. The engineer fell to the room's floor, his limbs twisted under him.

The only evidence of life was a faint crackle coming over his communicator: "Second engineer. . . we need confirmation of your last statement. Has station security been breached by agents from Vos? Second engineer, please respond. . ."

A full quarter of a time cycle after the small band of agents returned across the border into Vos, their explosives detonated, consuming Tarn's power station in a hideous fireball. Night turned to day and across the city, countless Autobots stared at the brilliant radiance that filled the horizon with mounting apprehension. . .

WAR!

Emirate Xaaron entered the celestial temple. Iacon's ruling council was deadlocked, and had been since Tarn declared war on Vos. However, the Autobot was determined that today's meeting would produce some positive action.

"How goes the war?" Tomaandi asked, as Xaaron entered the council room.

"It is as we suspected," Xaaron replied. "Agents from Vos' destroyed Tarn's power plant, and. . ."

"Yes. . . but there's been only minimal penetration of Vos' defence net and shock troops from both cities seem to cross the border indiscriminately."

"And the refugees," Tomaadi continued, "what of them?"

"They're being housed in various cities," Xaaron said. Autobots from both warring states had flooded into Iacon. They were offered fuel and shelter, but Xaaron was convinced that the refugees were only a symptom of a disease that the council had as yet failed to combat. He raised his head and looked across the council room. "General Traachon, I urge you once more to send a peace-keeping force to the war zone."

Traachon rose. "No!" he bellowed. "I will not allow an Iaconian force, peace-keeping or otherwise, to be caught in this conflict. Besides, have you considered that it's perhaps in our best interest if Vos and Tarn continue to destroy each other?"

DANGEROUS JOURNEY

Megatron looked out across the scarred wasteland that had once been his home city. Tarn held little for him now; his destiny lay in Iacon. It was only there that he could hope to create a power base large enough to fulfil his ambitions. Ambitions that would transform Cybertron into a mobile battle-station, which could then be used to establish a galaxy-wide empire. Megatron smiled, and was still smiling when Ravage approached.

"You find our situation amusing?" he asked.

"Oh," replied Megatron, "I find our situation amusing in the extreme!" and the gladiatorial champion of a dying city laughed long and loud at the twist of fate that had allied him to both Optimus Prime and the Autobot Overlord. Prime had been determined to escort the Overlord to the safety of Iacon, yet with the destruction of Tarn's power station, the only way to do so was by travelling through the central combat zone on foot. A treacherous journey at best, so recognizing safety in numbers, and having already decided to travel to Iacon himself, Megatron offered to help Prime in his endeavour.

The group's progress had been slow, hindered by frequent encounters with groups of shock troops and by the Overlord's constant need to re-charge his ageing circuits. But now they were nearing the border. One final expressway to cross and they would be safe inside Iacon's boundaries.

Megatron turned and stared at where the Overlord lay in the shadow of a building that had once been one of Tarn's border fortresses. The journey across the city had placed too great a strain on the Overlord's feeble circuits and he was undoubtedly now very close to death. Prime was bent low, administering what help he could to the aged Autobot.

This was the opportunity Megatron had been waiting for, and with cautious steps he began to negotiate the non-functioning bodies of the Autobot warriors that littered the expressway into Iacon. Maintaining a precarious balance, he managed to walk halfway across the gleaming structure before a weakened support shattered – producing a gaping hole in the expressway. There was no time to react and Megatron, all thoughts of war-worlds and galactic empires forgotten, found himself falling to Tarn's lower levels. The last thing he experienced before losing

consciousness was a sharp, tugging pain in his right arm.

RESCUE

Megatron awoke to see Prime standing above him.

"It was fortunate I was able to prevent your fall," the laconian said, his words tinged with contempt for Megatron's attempted desertion of the group. "For we'll need all our strength if we're to find an alternative route into lacon."

"I'm afraid that will be impossible."

Prime slowly turned to see Nightstalker approaching. "Why is that?" he asked.

"The Overlord cannot be moved just now. . . he'd never survive another journey."

"Then you three must remain here to guard him," Prime ordered. "I'll travel to lacon alone and return with help."

"But that will still take days," Nightstalker protested. "The Overlord is in need of immediate medical attention and. . ."

"I do not intend to try to map a different route into lacon." With that, Optimus turned, leapt over the hole in the expressway and was soon out of sight.

To Nightstalker Tarn had never seemed more peaceful. Before the war the city had teemed with life – boisterous and loud; yet now all seemed silent. It was a dealthy silence which reminded Nightstalker of the Overlord's deteriorating condition and he began to walk towards his master, hoping all the time that Prime would return.

An electron pistol suddenly flared in the darkness and almost simultaneously a high intensity laser beam melted Nightstalker's missile launcher.

"What – ?" Nightstalker raised his head and saw a small force of shock troops, members of Tarn's now all but defunct military, moving quickly towards him.

"Down!"

Nighstalker ducked and the first of the advancing shock troops were caught in a tremendous explosion. The smoke and debris cleared and the cat-like Transformer turned to see Megatron, a fusion cannon from one of the dead warriors on the expressway strapped to his arm. Ravage was standing by, his missiles primed and ready to launch.

"Quickly, move back! They'll re-group soon and attack a second time," Megatron bellowed.

FINAL MISSION

Time cycles passed and despite Megatron's deadly weapon, the group found themselves trapped between the shock troops and the impassable expressway.

"Ravage!" cried Megatron. "This is proving fruitless. Our only hope of survival lies in somehow bridging the hole in the expressway. "Are you with me?"

"No!" Nightstalker leapt into the pack of shock troops. "You can't abandon the Overlord now – you can't!"

The ancient bodyguard soon began to buckle beneath the troops' relentless blows and as an officer prepared to render Nightstalker non-functional, the entire group were destroyed in a thunderous explosion.

His eye circuits momentarily blinded, Megatron could do nothing but remain still. "What happened?" he whispered.

"A bomb," Ravage explained. "Quite a large bomb to be precise. All Overlord bodyguards are fitted with them. They're designed as a last line of defence. Most effective, don't you agree?"

"Help. . . please."

Forgotten in the heat of the battle, Megatron now walked over to the Overlord. "Yes?" he asked.

"Your energy. . . I need some of your energy," the dying Autobot begged. "Please, just until Prime returns. . . please."

"No, old one," Megatron sneered. "No energy for you!" He smiled a humourless smile. With the Overlord dead, there would be one less to oppose his future plans. And it would be easy to convince Prime and the other laconians that the shock of coming under attack had proved too much for the Overlord's weakened circuits. . .

The Autobot Overlord turned his gaze towards his bodyguard.

"Do not even consider asking the same of me," Ravage growled. "The balance of power on Cybertron is changing and I have chosen to ally myself with the planet's future ruler."

The final sight to greet the Overlord before becoming non-functional was Ravage slowly stalking over towards Megatron.

DANGEROUS DEVELOPMENTS

From his raised dais, Megatron gazed at the seemingly countless Autobots that crowded the auditorium – Autobots who had once been proud citizens of Vos and Tarn. But Vos and Tarn no longer existed. They had been consumed in the fiery light of two exploding photon missiles.

Megatron did not know what had led to both cities simultaneously launching Cybertron's 'ultimate deterrent'... he didn't care to know. All that mattered now was that the survivors of the war were united as never before. United in their feelings of hopelessness and frustration.

It had been such a simple task for Megatron to play upon this bitterness, to convince the refugees that Iacon could have ended the conflict, but had failed to do so. And it was with satisfaction that Megatron had learned that many of those gathered in front of him now believed Iacon had actually caused the war, in an attempt to be rid of its more powerful neighbour.

The ex-gladiator raised his arms and the restless crowd fell silent. "Our ranks have swollen, our stockpiles of weapons grown," he bellowed, "but still we must bide our time. From this day forward, we are not merely Transformers, we are not Autobots – we shall call ourselves Decepticons. And when they least expect it, we will have our revenge on the Iaconians!"

As he left the auditorium, Megatron could hear the roar of the crowded Decepticons. They were chanting a name. His name.

"Megatron! Megatron! Megatron!"

By James Hill

41

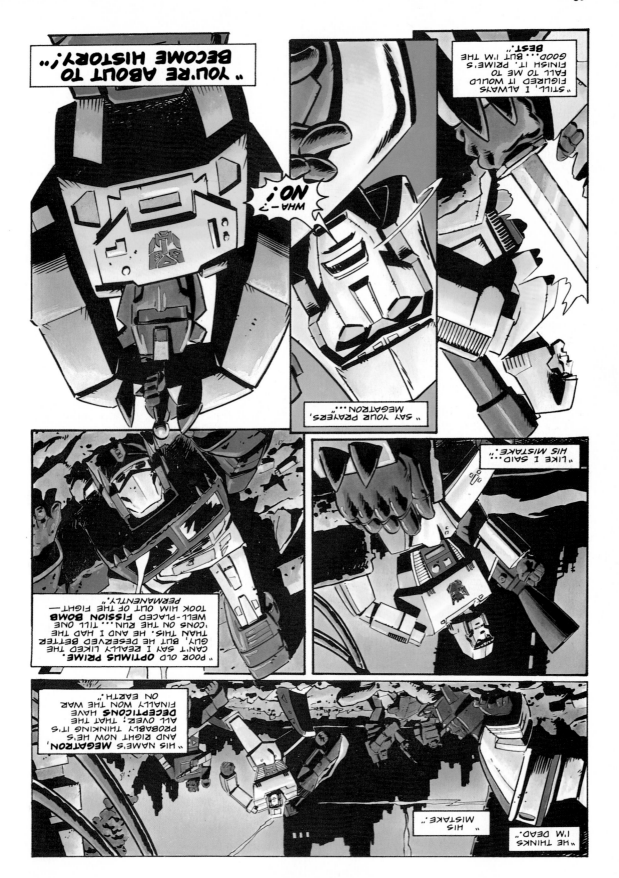

◀ VICTORY ▶

◄ VICTORY ►

◀ **VICTORY** ▶

"BEFORE MY WORLD **ERUPTS** IN FIRE AND LIGHT — DESCENDING INSTANTLY INTO..."

"DARKNESS."

"AND VOICES."

WELL, NOTHING. THAT'S WHAT I'M TRYING TO EXPLAIN.

"FREE!"

"AND ON THIS TERRAIN THE DECEPTICONS WILL NEVER TRAP ME AGAIN! I'VE WO--"

SLUDGE — STOP... PLEASE.

"THE HUMAN! THE BEAUTIFUL, SHINING HUMAN... SHE'S COME BACK TO ME!"

"THE DECEPTICONS TOOK HER FROM ME LAST TIME... TRICKED ME. I'LL NEVER LET THAT HAPPEN AGAIN!"

OH, SLUDGE — WELCOME BACK...

◄ **VICTORY** ►

48

VICTORY

◄ VICTORY ►

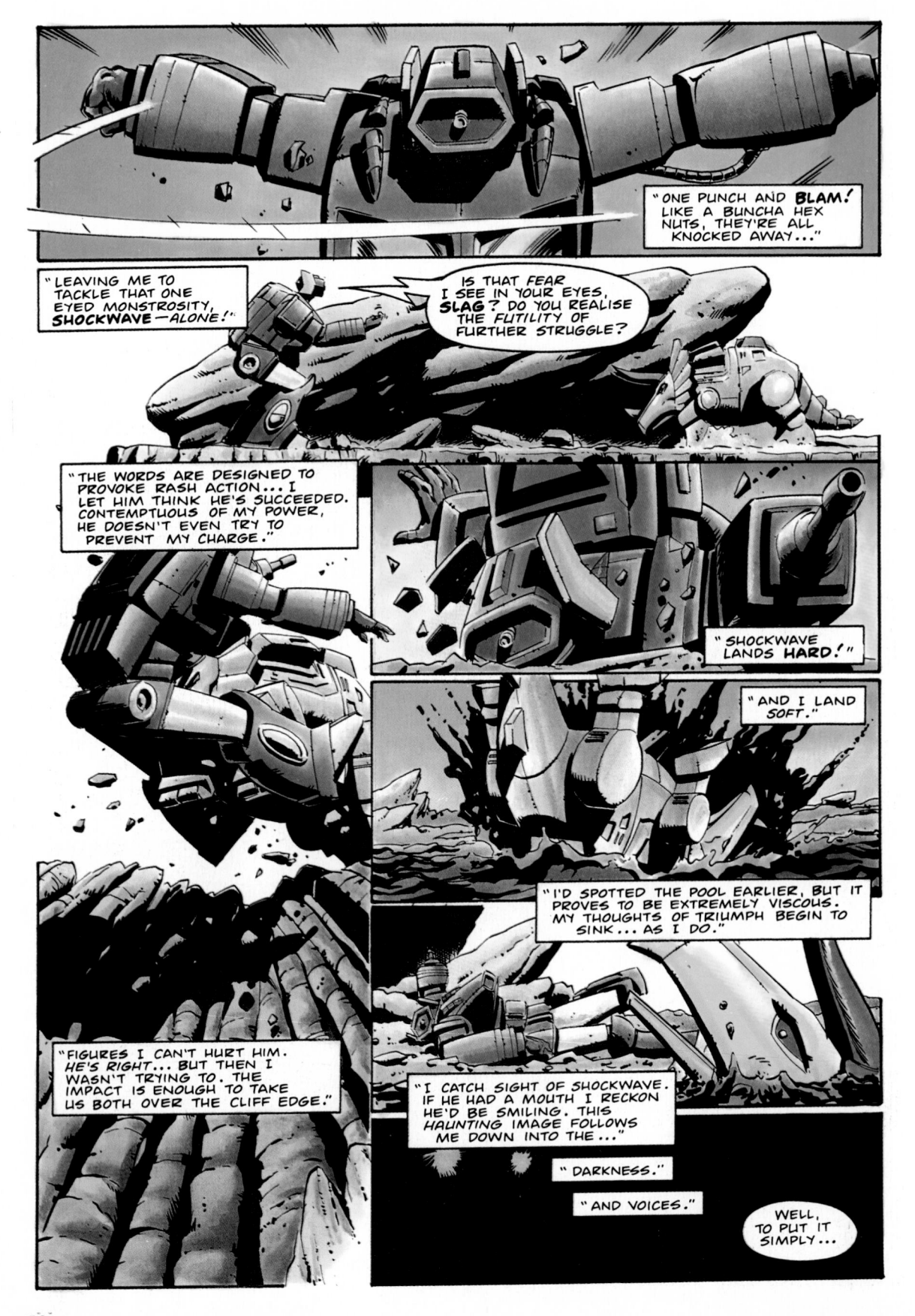

"ONE PUNCH AND **BLAM!** LIKE A BUNCHA HEX NUTS, THEY'RE ALL KNOCKED AWAY..."

"LEAVING ME TO TACKLE THAT ONE EYED MONSTROSITY, **SHOCKWAVE**—ALONE!"

IS THAT FEAR I SEE IN YOUR EYES, **SLAG**? DO YOU REALISE THE FUTILITY OF FURTHER STRUGGLE?

"THE WORDS ARE DESIGNED TO PROVOKE RASH ACTION... I LET HIM THINK HE'S SUCCEEDED. CONTEMPTUOUS OF MY POWER, HE DOESN'T EVEN TRY TO PREVENT MY CHARGE."

"SHOCKWAVE LANDS **HARD!**"

"AND I LAND SOFT."

"I'D SPOTTED THE POOL EARLIER, BUT IT PROVES TO BE EXTREMELY VISCOUS. MY THOUGHTS OF TRIUMPH BEGIN TO SINK... AS I DO."

"FIGURES I CAN'T HURT HIM. HE'S RIGHT... BUT THEN I WASN'T TRYING TO. THE IMPACT IS ENOUGH TO TAKE US BOTH OVER THE CLIFF EDGE."

"I CATCH SIGHT OF SHOCKWAVE. IF HE HAD A MOUTH I RECKON HE'D BE SMILING. THIS HAUNTING IMAGE FOLLOWS ME DOWN INTO THE..."

"DARKNESS."

"AND VOICES."

WELL, TO PUT IT SIMPLY...

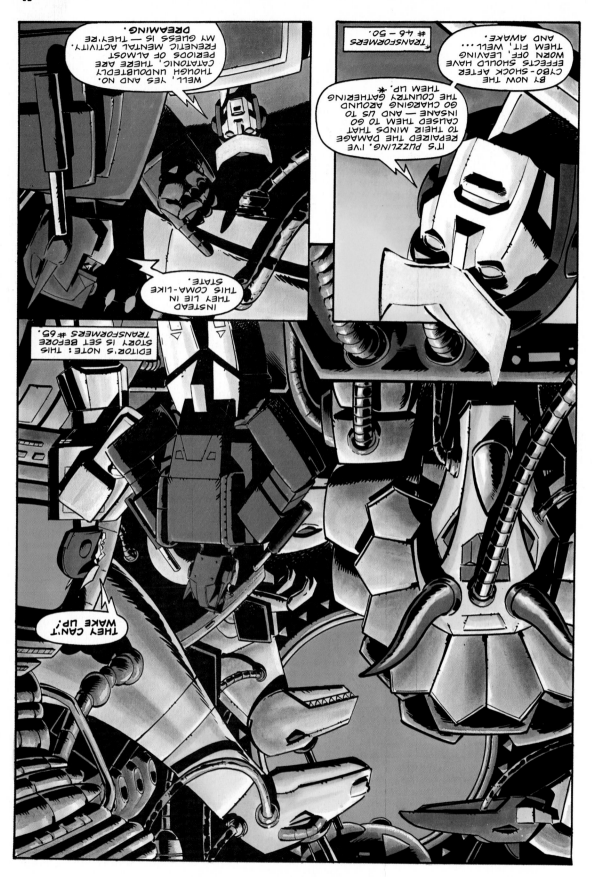

◄ VICTORY ►

LOOK AT THIS. THE **TRACE READING** SHOWS GRIMLOCK'S BRAIN WAVE ACTIVITY DURING AND AFTER HIS 'DREAM'.

WITHOUT THAT FINAL *MENTAL PUSH*, THEY STAY ASLEEP.

THE FEVER OF THE DREAM BUILDS STEADILY, TO A POINT WHICH WOULD NORMALLY RELEASE THE DREAMER FROM SLEEP.

BUT THEN, WITHOUT WARNING, IT DROPS RIGHT BACK TO ITS PREVIOUS LOW EBB.

AND IF THEY CONTINUALLY FAIL TO REACH THIS RELEASE POINT, WHAT THEN?

THE BRAIN'S DELICATE MECHANISMS BURN THEMSELVES OUT, AND YOU'RE LEFT WITH FIVE BLANK SLATES.

I CANNOT AFFORD TO LOSE THE DINOBOTS WITH SO MANY OF MY WARRIORS INJURED. **RATCHET** — YOU MUST FIND A WAY TO SAVE THEM!

IN SHORT — THEY DIE.

EASIER SAID THAN DONE, **PRIME**. I FEAR THERE IS NO WAY I CAN HELP THEM. SOME DEFECT IN THEIR PERSONALITY MAKE-UP MUST BE PREVENTING THEM FROM WAKING.

THIS IS ONE BATTLE THEY'RE GOING TO HAVE TO WIN FOR THEMSELVES.

AND IN THEIR DREAM-WORLD THE DINOBOTS GO TO WAR ONCE MORE...

GIVE THEM VICTORY — OR GIVE THEM DEATH!

THE END.

The MISSION

Their orders to spy on the Constructicons had been simple – then Hoist ran into trouble!

It was a monochrome world. The onset of the Alaskan winter had clapped the wild land in irons, squeezing the colour from the mountains and the sky. The black-toothed peaks chewed at grey clouds, swollen with snow.

Jazz, the heroic Autobot, was undismayed by the cold. He found the gigantic landscape exhilarating in its scale, its grandeur more a challenge than a threat. Although, in his current mode – disguised as a Porsche – the freezing conditions caused him some minor problems with traction.

He hugged himself closer to the frosted surface of the Alaskan highway and accelerated northwards. The road tested him as it writhed its way across the land. Jazz chased it, with the thrill of perfect control pulsing through him. He slid – broadsiding through the curves – and climbed through the howling gears, arrowing into the straights, cutting through an occasional brief convoy of toiling trucks, like a barracuda through a shoal of jellyfish. The stillness of the massive land invited speed – its silence, noise.

This landscape dwarfed even the Autobots, he thought. How it must oppress and torment the humans who came here! Their design allowed them only marginal resistance to temperature fluctuations. Thankfully, in this, as in most other aspects, Autobots were far superior machinery.

Jazz considered the force which drove him at such speed towards the heart of the Yukon region on the boundary between Canada and Alaska – the perpetual, Earthbound war with the Decepticons. This mission, on which he had embarked with his comrade, Hoist, should have been a straightforward one. A simple observation of the Con-structicons, perhaps rounded off with a bit of simple sabotage for good measure. However, something had gone drastically wong.

Jazz squeezed a few extra revolutions from his motor. He needed to hurry. There were still one hundred miles to cover before he must leave the road, then the same distance again across difficult terrain, to bring him to the origin point of Hoist's signal. He had not realised that their line of communications had become so extended. It was bad tactics. With enemies as dangerous as the Decepticons, mistakes could be costly.

ACTION AT LAST!

Despite a sense of foreboding, Jazz could not deny that the action was doing him good. He had been idle for too long. For three weeks he had been locked in a freight container. First there was a week, en route from San Francisco to Skagway by sea – a journey which had stressed his balance circuits severely. Then, a further two weeks in a Skagway freight yard, with all systems shut down to conserve fuel. Listening watch only, had been the orders – it had seemed like eternity. When, finally, the brief signal had found his eager antennae and tripped his systems into life, it had not been the one he was expecting. It had been a single brief transmission on the Autobots' Urgent Distress Frequency.

Hoist had done good work as a scout in the past, Jazz had thought as, gunning his powerful motor fiercely, he had cracked out of the steel container as if it were tinfoil; but he lacked flair. He was too methodical for fieldwork. He was a workshop machine, maintainance was his strength. However, with the Decepticons fighting on so many different

53

fronts, the Autobot warriors were spread too thinly. All hands were pressed into service; constant opposition to the enemy was vital. Now Hoist had got himself into trouble. Jazz hoped that his comrade had not tangled with the Constructicons. They would turn him into scrap and use him to make rivets.

Like a snarling bullet, the Porsche ripped into the sub-arctic night. In his riotous wake, snakes of powdered snow writhed, hissing from the road.

SHREWD TACTICS

Until he had stepped into the hole, Hoist had been well satisfied with progress of his mission. It had been no easy task to locate and observe the enemy unit in such haphazard and gargantuan geography as that of the Yukon territory. A city could be lost and never found here. But by shrewd tactics and thoroughly practised techniques he had accomplished his task.

He had tracked the Constructicons and for three days he had waited motionless in the dark, cold, shadows of the mountainside. Only his powerful full-spectrum scanners operated in this time — locked onto the activity of the Constructicons, as constantly they mined and tunnelled their way into the permanently deep-frozen silt of the river plain below.

Whether it was a tactical base they were building, or a mine for some kind of mineral fuel source, Hoist had been unable to ascertain from long range. So, as the Constructicons had now become invisible to his sensory receptors — other than as a clatter of indistinguishable industry beneath the surface of the ice-bound ground — he had deduced that the risk involved in a covert, close-quarters reconnaissance of the target was acceptable.

He had raised his massive bulk to a vertical position. Ice which had lacquered him burst away from his flexing joints in small crystal explosions as the Autobot manoeuvred his frosted form down towards the terraces of the frozen flood-plain.

Conscious of his high sensor profile in this open country, Hoist had kept low, hugging the occasional rocky shoulder with which the mountains nudged the ice-skirted streams towards the river. In this fashion he had approached to within half-a-mile of the enemy's subterranean work site.

DISASTER!

Then, crossing a low ridge-top with all sensors locked firmly onto the target — alert for the sudden, searing light of a laser — waiting for the rush and metal-tearing fire of a missile — Hoist had stepped forward into nothing. Sudden, split-second, bottomless, unknown, nothing.

With a gyro-wrenching jolt the drop had stopped short and Hoist was trapped, suspended, held by the shoulders in the impossible grip of the earth frozen hard as granite. His huge legs had flailed at emptiness in wild, futile, energy expenditure and his torso had flexed and strained against the immovable walls of the pit into which he had fallen. Then came realisation that a moment of carelessness had brought potential disaster on him and his mission.

He had fallen into some kind of vertical shaft — not a natural feature — and was now wedged with his arms trapped uselessly by his sides. Worst of all, his head and the armoured dome of his shoulders were sticking up above the surface of the ground, like a beacon for the first Constructicon who surfaced for a routine defensive scan. He had decided to risk a brief emergency transmission, calculating that even if the enemy intercepted his signal and destroyed him, Jazz would still have the target's location.

As the frozen hours passed, there was wind. With the wind came snow — swarming out of the darkness liked crazed bees. The Autobot scout waited. He could do nothing else.

ROUGH TERRAIN

After leaving the Alaskan highway and enduring twenty miles of cratered dirt road, until the risk of mechanical damage began to outweigh the benefits of speed, Jazz reluctantly abandoned his Porsche mode and transformed.

There had followed eight hours of slow, zig-zag navigation through a savage landscape. He had climbed boulder-strewn mountain passes and ploughed, stumbling through drifted fields of snow. The wind drove constant flights

of ice needles which scoured him abrasively, periodically clogging his sensory receptors, blinding and disorientating him as he struggled to make his way towards the source of the distress signal.

His sensors determined the location of the Constructicons easily enough. Briefly he considered a lightning, maximum fire-power strike on the concealed installation. But however tempting the prospect of entombing the Constructicons in a crypt of their own manufacture, Jazz's priority had had to be to ascertain the fate of Hoist. He thought he detected traces of Autobot alloys – but the geometry of the image was wrong.

Apprehensively he went to full scanner power and focused. Out on the snow carpet he now distinguished the head and shoulders of his comrade. The Constructicons must have destroyed him and left this wreckage as a warning – or a trap. Fascination and dread drew Jazz down onto his belly and he furrowed forward through the snow, armour grinding on the hard ground beneath. His weaponry was ranged and armed.

As he drew near to the remains of Hoist, he was fine-tuned to a hair trigger of violent reaction, expecting a Constructicon ambush at any second. So, when suddenly his comrade's head swivelled towards him and spoke, it was unfortunate, but not surprising, that Jazz reacted in the way that he did.

Hoist had remained completely still as the snow hurried down around him, covering his body and the pit. Once more he had shut down all systems except for perception, to minimise the chances of detection by the enemy and to conserve fuel. When, eventually, he sensed movement behind him he knew that it must be Jazz. Gratefully he turned to greet him.

RELEASED

His comrade's action was spontaneous – and ultimately disastrous. At the sound of Hoist's voice, Jazz flipped over in a blur of motion. He snapped into an attack position and Hoist saw the Autobot's photon-rifle lurch as it discharged a concentrated gem of solar power into the Constructicon position.

"Why?" Hoist asked, bewildered. "Why did you do that?"

As soon as he had fired, Jazz realised he had responded more like an untested junior warrior on his first mission, than a hardened Autobot commander. He had jeopardised their position in the extreme. He recovered his equilibrium and sprang into action. Straddling the pit, he bent and thrust down his arms to find firm purchase on the smooth, hard armour of the trapped Autobot. Enormous feet chewed into the frozen ground as machinery stressed and levered. Jazz increased power to maximum and, slowly, the dead weight of Hoist began to lift from the pit.

"Trust you to come all this way without mishap and then to fall into a gold-mine at the last minute!"

"Gold-mine?" replied Hoist, as his shoulder armour screamed in friction with the rock-hard earth.

"Do you mean that humans would endure these conditions to dig a useless metal from the ground. . ."

"They have no logic."

Jazz would have liked to explain what he had learned of the Klondike gold rushes. How hundreds of thousands of men and women forced their way into the wilderness – enduring misery upon misery, deprivation upon deprivation – in order to win riches and respect. But he knew that Hoist would not understand – and the time was inappropriate.

With an ungainly metallic slithering, the bulk of the freed Autobot tangled him into the snow. Jazz extricated himself and was about to suggest that they made a hasty strategic withdrawal when he was distracted by a sudden prickle of light from the enemy position. He barely had time to acknowledge this as laser fire, when the world turned red and then disappeared in a flare of purest sterile white.

Clumsily rolling into an operating position, Hoist saw and felt the vicious lines of laser light cutting the air and boiling into the snow around them. Instinctively, he returned fire, his arm launching a covering pattern of heat-seeking missiles which charged, vapour trailing behind them, into the enemy emplacement. He looked for Jazz — and was dismayed to see him stationary and fully exposed to the Constructicon fire. Hoist's expert eye scanned for damage — and found it. Jazz had been hit in the side of the head.

The armoured steel, still glowing faintly, was puckered around a small, neat puncture. Hoist knew that the Autobot's sensory and logistical circuits — a complex honeycomb of micro-circuitry — must have been powdered by this hot-shot.

The Constructicons were fanning out, trying to surround them before moving in to finish them off. Hoist had to get both of them into concealment, or a strong defensive position — or they were doomed.

Fortunately, although Jazz's logic circuits had been re-structured by the laser, his motor mechanisms were unimpaired. Bellowing wildly, Hoist bundled him frantically towards the sheltering slopes of the dark mountainside. With fortune and the inaccuracy of the Constructicon marksmen, they might just make it before they were overrun. . .

CONFUSION

Abruptly, he was aware that he had been moving for a long time.

Who was he? Where was he? Why was he?

What was that thunderous voice that roared in his head? Why was he being pushed, slipping, sliding, crashing and reeling through the jagged black and soft white of this place?

On a ridge-top, he stopped and turned to consider his tormentor, a powerful machine of destruction and violence. He struggled to frame intelligible sounds, but a siren wail that seemed to mimic the wind was all that burst from him. Simultaneously, a splash of fire blossomed beside them, throwing out shoots of rock and ice which rattled and punched at his metallic hide.

He was still listening to the complex percussion of the falling debris, when the violent machine swung a mighty arm and struck him a ringing blow. Surprised and unbalanced, he toppled and fell, limbs scrabbling wildly for grip where there was none. Then he was moving, accelerating downwards in a reckless exhilaration of speed, cleaving up plumes of soft, white powder. He was out of control.

"Move! Move!" Hoist roared in frustration. His damaged comrade stood, vacant, as if engrossed in some strange entertainment. Hoist shoved him again, as he had been shoving him for hour after mountainous hour, mile after ice-bound mile, trying desperately to keep ahead of the pursuing Constructicons.

He watched for a second as Jazz tobogganed down the ice-slope and then, spurred on by the laser fire that pierced and shattered the black rock around him, he too launched himself on the armour-rattling descent.

If Hoist's navigation was correct they should have cleared the high peaks now and should soon be able to make the tree-line and find forest cover. Fifteen hundred feet below, he came abruptly to rest at the foot of the ice-slope. He shook free the snow that had compacted itself in his scanners and looked for his hapless companion. Locating him, Hoist groaned inwardly — more aberrant behaviour!

The second-in-command of the Autobot Warriors, right-hand of the great Optimus Prime, was sitting atop a large snow-clad boulder — his attention rapt upon six balls of compacted snow, which he manipulated skilfully from hand to hand, managing to keep them all airborne and mobile.

Juggling. In the midst of a potential battle-zone, he was juggling! Still, at least there was nothing wrong with his co-ordination, thought Hoist.

COVER AT LAST

After several miles of difficult descent through a boulder-choked gully, they entered the forest.

Hoist felt marginally more secure as they moved between the trees. They would help screen them from the Constructicon scanners. His damaged companion, Jazz, seemed to be inhabiting a different world. He had lost all awareness of their mission and the danger they were in. He sauntered along, stopping to investigate every feature of their environment in minute detail, as if each held the secrets of the Universe. It was highly tedious and Hoist wasted critical fuel in constantly prodding the Autobot onwards.

Hoist had calculated that their fuel reserves would not take them beyond reach of the enemy. They were going to need transport. A vague plan was forming in his logic centres. He knew that, mathematically, its chances of success were slim; but the only alternative was ultimate destruction at the hands of the Constructicons. They must press on to the south. They needed a river.

Simultaneous with the awareness of a distant crashing and shattering of timber which assailed his senses, Hoist realised that Jazz was no longer with him. Desperately he scanned, trying to locate his comrade's metal bulk amongst the distracting ghost images thrown back by the trees.

Jazz sat as if sculpted from the landscape. His attention was wholly focused on a stunningly perfect piece of machinery. Four delicately precise limbs supported a powerful, lithe, brown torso. The head, set atop a strong flexible neck, bore strange, spreading antennae with which, for some mysterious purpose, it scraped at the column of one of the tall, static machines.

Suddenly, the entrancing machine froze. Briefly, it cocked its head to one side and then was gone. Disappointed, he turned to find the Violent One shouldering his way through the densely packed columns, like an avalanche.

DEVASTATOR!

Hoist knew from the scale and volume of the fast closing pursuit that the Constructicons must have combined into their awesome composite form – Devastator. Frantically he bullied the unwilling Jazz through the clawing forest. He was urged both by the horrendous tearing of timber, as the gargantuan Decepticon machine levelled all before it in its single-minded desire to annihilate them – and by the fact that he sensed the presence of water ahead.

In seconds they broke from the trees and stood on the rocky banks of a river.

Instantly Hoist was assailed by doubt. A hundred yards upstream the towering, curved, concrete wall of what he recognised to be a hydro-electric dam spanned the river gorge. What should have been a violent torrent was reduced to a sedate surge. Surely the water would not have depth or power enough for his purpose. Nevertheless, with Devastator's ruthless destruction of the forest rending the mountain air, he knew that defeat could not be contemplated. They were Heroic Autobots – the conflict would continue to the end.

Quickly Hoist selected four tall, thick pine trees. With a series of rapid, powerful movements, he felled and stripped them of branches. Then he manipulated them into the water. It was barely deep enough to float them.

Hoist sensed that the end was near. They would have to stand and fight.

Fifty yards downstream, the mighty form of Devastator ripped, splintering out of the forest. Remorselessly it scanned the river gorge for its enemies. Hoist primed his weaponry and looked for Jazz. In full view, the damaged Autobot was standing, facing the soaring wall of the dam, calmly scanning it from to to botom and from side to side.

CAUGHT IN THE OPEN

Ugly, he thought to himself. This wall was ugly. It should not be here, obstructing the flow of the water. The water was a part of the big machine that was this planet. The planet was part of the solar system and that was part. . . The wall was wrong.

Sounds from behind turned him. Two things were happening. The Violent One who harrassed him constantly, was approaching at speed and beyond him a gigantic machine straddled the river, crushing boulders to powder under its enormous weight. This giant was pointing at him.

Then the Violent One cannoned into him, slamming him back into the ugly concrete of the wall. At the same moment, from the pointing arm of the giant machine, a light flared out, like the light of suns. Energy crackled past him and solid heat chewed into the wall, concentrating on a patch which suddenly spurted water and steam in a glittering power-jet.

Then the Violent One was dragging him again. The pulsing light danced from the giant's arm several more times but it did not touch them. The Violent One reached suddenly for his head – and then there was nothing at all.

FINAL CHANCE

There was a chance, one final, desperate chance. Hoist saw it and took it. The ten-thousand degree pulse of solar energy which Devastator had launched at Jazz had punched a hole straight through the dam. Hoist saw cracks, beginning as filaments but rapidly spreading into a web which crumbled from its centre. He knew that he had but scant seconds.

He dragged Jazz to where the tree-trunks bobbed and lurched, side by side on the slowly rising river. With the quick, deft skill of an expert mechanic, he shut down Jazz's systems completely. He just had time to lay the disabled Autobot on the loose raft and throw himself on top – clenching and binding the tree-trunks together with his own huge strength – before the dam disintegrated.

A mighty, surging roar of water boiled into the river gorge and plucked up the cumbersome vessel like a feather, spinning and tossing it forward in a wild freedom of escape.

An image, which would remain in Hoist's memory banks for ever, swept by. In panic and alarm, the Constructicons had disassembled from their Devastator mode as the churning wall of water spewed over them. In a split second they were submerged – bowled and scraped along the bottom of the gorge like pebbles – whilst the Autobots' raft surfed over them on wild wings of water.

The mission was over, thought Hoist. They had failed, but not completely. The war would continue and he and his comrade Jazz, repaired by Ratchet, would fight the Decepticons again.

Two days later, at a back-road gas-station, just south of the Canadian border, a sleepy pump-jockey was surprised to see a towtruck towing a battered Porsche that looked as if it had been in the wars. He was more surprised, as he watched them disappear down the road, to realise that it had no driver.

By Jamie Delano.

THE DECEPTICON

We are proud to present an up-to-the-minute guide to the ranks of the evil Decepticons (storywise, rather than toy-wise) with accompanying information on each member's abilities, function, rank and current status. It's an invaluable companion to the continuing adventures of The Transformers . . .

DECEPTICON LEADERS

SHOCKWAVE
Current Decepticon Commander. Status – missing, but presumed still functional. Usurped command of the Decepticons from Megatron after defeating him in battle. Transforms into a giant ray-gun and controls energy in a wide variety of forms, emitting that energy as powerful force beams.

MEGATRON
Former Decepticon Commander. Status – missing, presumed destroyed following his battle with the Autobot, Ratchet, and the Dinobots. Uses his fusion cannon in the absence of both Megatron and Shock-wave. Ceaselessly monitors the airwaves for information, picks up the slightest sound, and reads minds by monitoring electrical brain impulses.

SPY CASSETTES

FRENZY
Creates high-pitched sonic blasts and craves only to spread fear and destruc-tion.

RUMBLE
His piledriving arms create mini-earthquakes and can pound a foe mercilessly.

SOUNDWAVE
Communications Officer. Status – acting Commander of the Decepticons in the absence of both Megatron and Shock-wave. Ceaselessly monitors the airwaves for information, picks up the slightest sound, and reads minds by monitoring electrical brain impulses.

RAVAGE
Resembles Earth's Jaguar in robot form. He is a master spy; stealthy and cunning.

LASERBEAK
Resembles Earth's Condor. A specialist in interrogation with his high-power optical lasers.

MEGATRON
Former Decepticon Commander. Status – missing, presumed destroyed following his battle with the Autobot, Ratchet, and the Dinobots. Uses his fusion cannon in the form of a P-38 robot form and in the form of a P-38 pistol. The strongest Decepticon.

BUZZSAW
The twin of Laserbeak. His diamond-hard, micro-serrated beak can carve up any opponent.

JET PLANES

STARSCREAM
Aerospace Commander. Ruthless and cold-blooded, he wishes only to over-throw the Decepticon Commander and take control.

SKYWARP
Possesses the ability to teleport in mid-flight.

THUNDERCRACKER
Can unleash an ear-splitting sonic boom.

THE CONSTRUCTICONS

SCAVENGER
Power Shovel. Function – mining and construction.

SCRAPPER
Tractor Shovel. Function – construction engineer.

MIXMASTER
Concrete Mixer. Function – fabrication of materials.

HOOK
Truck Crane. Function – surgical en-gineer.

LONG HAUL
Dump Truck. Function – transport of goods.

BONECRUSHER
Bulldozer. Function – demolition.

THE AUTOBOT

WHO'S WHO

we are equally proud to present the definitive guide to all the heroic Autobots currently battling within these pages. This two-part reference wall-chart has information on each member's abilities, functions, rank and current status.

HIGH COMMAND

JAZZ
Joint second-in-command. Status — injured; undergoing treatment. Transforms into a Porsche, and specialises in dangerous sabotage missions. Good knowledge of Earth culture.

OPTIMUS PRIME
Autobot Commander. Status — active. Transforms into a tractor trailer — though this is in truth three independent modules. *Brain centre* has vast strength and a laser rifle, *Roller* is the spy unit, and *Combat Deck* stores artillery and radiation weapons. Injury to one module is felt by the other two.

PROWL
Joint second-in-command. Status — active. Transforms into police patrol car. Specialises in military strategy.

TECHNICIANS

JETFIRE
Aerospace Commander. Status — active. Transforms into a Valkyrie jet-fighter. Specialises in technological advancement.

RATCHET
Chief Medical Officer. Honorary member of the High Command. Status — active. Transforms into an ambulance.

IRONHIDE
Security Officer. Status — active. Transforms into a transit van.

WHEELJACK
Chief Mechanical Engineer. Status — active. Specialises in inventions and hardware. Transforms into a Lancia sports car.

GRAPPLE
Architect. Status — active. Transforms into a Truck Crane.

HOIST
Maintenance. Status — active. Transforms into a Tow-truck.

MIRAGE
Military Intelligence Officer. Status — active. Transforms into racing car. Possesses the ability to project images of himself.

DINOBOTS

GRIMLOCK
Dinobot Commander. Status — injured; undergoing treatment. Resembles a

SLAG
Flamethrower. Status — injured; undergoing treatment. Resembles a Tricera-

SWOOP
Aerial Commando. Status — injured; undergoing treatment. Resembles a Pter-

SLUDGE
Jungle Warrior. Status — injured; undergoing treatment. Resembles a Bronto-

SNARL
Desert Warrior. Status — injured; undergoing treatment. Resembles a Stego-